INDIRECT METHOD

Books by Francis King

NOVELS

To the Dark Tower
Never Again
An Air that Kills
The Dividing Stream
The Dark Glasses
The Firewalkers (under the
pseudonym of Frank Cauldwell)
The Widow
The Man on the Rock
The Custom House
The Last of the Pleasure Gardens
The Waves Behind the Boat
A Domestic Animal
Flights
A Game of Patience
The Needle
Danny Hill (editor)
The Action

SHORT STORIES

So Hurt and Humiliated
The Japanese Umbrella
The Brighton Belle
Hard Feelings

POETRY

Rod of Incantation

BIOGRAPHY

E. M. Forster and his World

Francis King

INDIRECT METHOD
And Other Stories

Hutchinson
London Melbourne Sydney Auckland Johannesburg

Hutchinson & Co. (Publishers) Ltd

An imprint of the Hutchinson Publishing Group

3 Fitzroy Square, London W I P 6JD

Hutchinson Group (Australia) Pty Ltd
30–32 Cremorne Street, Richmond South, Victoria 3121
P O Box 151, Broadway, New South Wales 2007

Hutchinson Group (N Z) Ltd
32–34 View Road, P O Box 40–086, Glenfield, Auckland 10

Hutchinson Group (S A) (Pty) Ltd
P O Box 337, Bergvlei 2012, South Africa

This selection first published 1980
© Francis King 1980

Set in Monotype Fournier

Printed in Great Britain by The Anchor Press Ltd
and bound by Wm Brendon & Son Ltd
both of Tiptree, Essex

British Library Cataloguing in Publication Data

King, Francis
    Indirect method, and other stories
    I. Title
    823'.9'1FS   PR6061.I45I/

ISBN 0 09 143690 7

Contents

Indirect Method	9
The Wake	33
Sundays	47
The Glass House	58
Blindness	78
Unmaking	85
Love's Old Sweet Song	101
The Stepson's Story	108
Little Old Lady Passing By	140
Appetites	158
Voices	170

Acknowledgements

The following stories first appeared as indicated and the author and publishers acknowledge with thanks the permission of the publishers concerned to reproduce them in this volume: The Wake in *London Magazine*, The Stepson's Story in *Winter's Tales*, Appetite in *Encounter* and Voices in *The New Review*.

Indirect Method

THIS is a room. What is this?

It is a room.

This is a hotel room. What kind of room is this?

It is a hotel room.

This is an expensive room – the most expensive room in which I have ever stayed. Is this room expensive?

Yes, it is expensive.

Direct Method. Liz hears Mildred's voice or the ghost of Mildred's voice (so long silent, letters to Canada unanswered, perhaps Mildred dead) teaching her pupils in the dining-room.

Who is Mildred?

Mildred is the teacher.

She is (was) also the lodger, who had come out to Japan with an Air Force husband, had abandoned him or been abandoned by him (the story changed as rapidly and inexplicably as her spirits would soar or sink) and had then set up as a freelance teacher.

Direct Method. But Mildred said that people as indirect as the Japanese did not take to it. They preferred word-for-word translation. Fish have neither hands nor feet – *Sakana niwa te mo ashi mo arimasen.* That kind of thing. Mildred swore that she had seen that sentence in a course for beginners prepared by some Japanese professor. But so many of the strange or exciting things that Mildred related had happened only in her imagination. Perhaps (Tom and Liz sometimes speculated) the marriage to the Air Force officer had also happened only there.

This is a room. This is a hotel room. This is an expensive room.

There are two beds, each neatly folded down to make a white

sandwich-like triangle at either corner. There are two armchairs
and two bedside tables, each with a lamp on it and each with a
Gideon Bible in its drawer. In the bathroom there are two face
towels and two bath towels and two glasses which have a paper
seal over them, like the paper seals over the bidet and lavatory
bowl.

I expect you wish to be left alone, Professor Ito told her down
in the lobby. The truth is that Professor Ito wished to leave her
alone, because he wished to get back to his laboratory, even
though it was already past nine. You must be tired and tomorrow
your programme is a busy one. He finds it hard to adjust to the
fact that the young, untidy woman with all those children, who
used to work up at the Baptist Hospital, should now be a leading
authority on diabetes. In the past he patronized her, as he
patronized her husband, also a doctor. He wants to continue to
patronize her but feels, baffled and slightly exasperated, that he
can no longer do so.

Liz does not really want to be left alone, because to be alone,
except when she is working, is something to which she is not
accustomed. If the room were less expensive, she might hear
sounds from the rooms on either side of her: the flush of a
lavatory, the throbbing of a radio, voices raised in anger or in
love. But this is an expensive room.

The walls are covered in shimmering grey silk, so that, in the
lamplight, they look as if cooling water were trickling down
them; but, in fact, the coolness comes from the air-conditioner
grill, from which a strand of pale blue ribbon streams outwards
to show that it is functioning. There is a darker grey silk covering
the lampshades, and the thick carpet is of the same colour. There
is a crimson-and-white *toile de Jouy* on the chairs and the
headboards of the beds, and the curtains are of the same material.
The design, of a woman on a swing, her skirts billowing up
around her, while a courtier kneels and plays some kind oı
stringed instrument, suggests a Fragonard.

Liz begins to unpack. She has travelled on the bullet train
from Tokyo and she feels as though she herself had been shot by

some invisible gun through all those hundreds and hundreds of miles, to arrive, blunted and bruised, on this target. She feels no hunger, only an insistent thirst. In the bathroom she has seen a little spigot, with assurances in Japanese, English, French and German, that the water is both drinkable and iced. She breaks the seal of the glass and fills it. Then, in the room with no climate, she drinks the water with no taste. The air is filtered, the water is filtered. The cold rim of the now empty glass against her lips, she stares at the television set. It has a blind across it, not of the *toile de Jouy* but of a crimson velvet, as though something obscene might be going on, unseen, on its screen.

She will ring Yamada-san, she will ring Mrs Payne at the Baptist Hospital, she will ring the Bensons, she will ring Yoshiko. . . . No, she will do none of those things. Not yet. But she will ring Osamu.

The telephone has the texture and colour of mother-of-pearl. Oh, Osamu, she would say, do please try to get this number for me. These Japanese phones drive one round the bend. But this one works perfectly. It is a woman who answers (*'Moshi! Moshi!'*) and of course that must be Osamu's wife, whom Liz has never met but whose colour photograph she has seen, beautiful in a kimono with a dragon writhing up one side.

One moment! Please!

Osamu's wife, Noriko, must know who she is. She sounds excited.

Mrs Butler . . . Osamu is giggling with pleasure. You have come at last!

This was our houseboy. Who was he?

He was your houseboy.

He learned English by the Direct Method. He learned it by talking it to us and the children. He did not learn it from Mildred or any school.

Osamu wants to come round to the hotel immediately; but Liz still has that feeling that she has been fired from a gun, it is now almost ten, and she knows, because he has written to tell her, that he now lives in a remote suburb out near Arashiyama.

Tomorrow, she says. And he says, Yes, tomorrow, he will call in on his way to the office.

That means, since this is Japan and not England, that he will call in at half past seven.

You can have some breakfast with me.

He is not sure about that; but he will call in.

They sat at the breakfast table and Osamu sat with them. That was in the last months, not when he first came to them and sat in the kitchen. Even when he sat with them, he liked to have rice and pickles for breakfast. The pickles had a pungent, slightly rotten smell that Tom would say, in private, put him off his food. Osamu also made himself soup for breakfast, pouring hot water onto powder from a packet and then slurping it noisily. Tom said that that slurping put him off his food too.

Liz replaces the telephone on its cradle. There is a throbbing at her temples and, though she has just drunk that glass of iced water, her mouth and even her throat already feel dry. It must be the air-conditioning. Or nerves. Only now does she notice that, under a bank of drawers of the built-in furniture, there is a small refrigerator. It will be stacked with bottles that she will never open.

The *toile-de-Jouy* curtains are drawn back, in such perfectly symmetrical folds that either the maid must have spent minutes arranging them like that or else they are never closed. Beyond them, instead of an ordinary window, there is an exquisite *shoji* – a frame of delicate blond wood, each of its squares filled with a nacreous paper that perfectly matches the telephone. It is so silent in this room that she wonders what lies behind the *shoji*. Some miniature garden, devotedly tended by a wizened man with the legs of an ancient boiling fowl? (Osamu raked the garden with fierce rhythmical strokes.) Some tributary of the Kamogawa river, with a hump-back bridge and willows drooping their splayed fingers along its margins? (Osamu, flushed and slightly unsteady from two whiskies, leant beside her over the parapet, squinting down into the barely moving water.)

Liz crosses to the window. PLEASE DO NOT OPEN. The prohibition is there in English and, of course, like every other instruction in the room, also in Japanese, French and German. But she must get it open, she must see what lies behind it. She struggles and at last, squeaking in its grooves, the *shoji* begins to slide away.

Four – five? – feet away from her is a high, totally blank wall. She puts her head out, twists it uncomfortably, tries to crane upwards. There is a plume of smoke at the top, which uncurls and then slowly dissipates. She looks down. Far below, there is a cobbled alley, but she cannot make out where it comes from or where it goes.

She pulls the *shoji* back again. She must forget that she ever disobeyed the prohibition to open it. She must forget that blank wall and the strange plume of smoke at the top. She must forget that alley, which seems a passageway too narrow for anything but rats. She must still imagine that miniature garden or that tributary of the river or even a view of distant Mount Hiei, where Osamu pointed, Look, Mrs Butler! A monkey! Many monkeys! and there they were, grey and shrilly chattering, as they swung themselves from liana to liana and from branch to branch.

She must keep calm. She must have no claustrophobia. No one could stifle in a room like this, so long as that pale blue ribbon streams out from the grill of the air conditioner.

This is a room. What is this?

It is a prison.

No, this is a room. This is an expensive room. What is this?

It is a prison.

Osamu wore wooden clogs, an open-necked aertex shirt (one of Tom's cast-offs) and a pair of jeans with a St Martin label. He wears black brogues, a network of tiny cracks across their insteps, a blue pin-stripe suit, the trousers of which are short enough to reveal his dark-blue hose with their scarlet clocks on them, and a white polythene shirt with a dark blue tie, the knot of which has the explosive appearance of a bud that is about to burst open. Osamu had hair cropped so close to his head that you could see the scalp. His hair is now brushed back from an incision-like parting and it is heavily greased. Osamu was handsome. He is handsome.

You have not changed at all, he says. Fifteen, sixteen years! Just the same!

But they have both changed. Her hair is greying and she has an air of quiet authority that he finds as disconcerting as she finds his sudden attacks of giggling.

Have some coffee. Tea? Something? Anything?

But he shakes his head and looks at his watch, as, across the table from him, she fiddles with the cutlery. He is afraid of being late at the office, though he was often late for her and Tom.

He now asks about Tom and the children, laughing incredulously when she tells him that Anna is married and has a baby, that Adrienne is now at Oxford, and that Jerry now plays cricket for his school. All these things have been recorded in the occasional letters she has written to him. She now wonders if he has ever read those letters, as she has always read his.

He looks again at his watch. It is a multifunctional, digital one, and she knows what Tom's verdict would be on it: Vulgar. It has a gold bracelet but she doubts if the gold is gold all through.

Mrs Butler . . .

She smiles and corrects him: Liz.

Liz . . . But he finds that difficult. He has to go, he says. He has to open up the office, it is he who has the keys. No, no, she must not get up from the table, she must continue with her breakfast.

But she follows him out into the foyer, where he tells her: I will see you on Saturday. A statement, not a question. He adds: Unfortunately, every weekday I am busy.

I am busy on weekdays too. Professor Ito has already given her her programme, a sheet for each day, with the sheets all stapled together inside a cardboard cover to make what looks like a paperback.

I will bring my car and we can go wherever you wish.

Your car! You have a car now?

He giggles. Very old, he says.

Osamu usually drove the car for them, because Tom hated negotiating those narrow alleys, and she had still to learn. He liked to drive fast, to prevent bigger cars from overtaking, to overtake bigger cars. He had a number of minor accidents, until Tom threatened to deduct the cost of the next from his wages; but each repair bill was far in excess of what they paid him for a month.

She presses a handkerchief to her upper lip, saying: So early in the morning and yet already it is hot.

He tells her to please go back to her breakfast but, tactless, she insists: she must see this car of his.

In the hotel carpark there are a number of American limousines among the new or almost new Toyotas and Datsuns and Hondas. A Japanese, in a gleaming white, short-sleeved shirt, jeans and rubber gloves is washing down a bronze Rolls-Royce with a CD number-plate.

Osamu repeats: My car is very old.

It looks to her like any car in any street in London; but then, scrutinizing it more carefully, she sees that, yes, there are signs of rust here and there.

It is all I can afford, he tells her.

I can't see anything wrong with it. We have an absolutely ancient Mini to run around in. She does not mention that she and Tom also have a brand-new Peugeot.

I will call for you on Saturday. About eleven. A statement, not a question.

Lovely. A statement too. It is really for him and not for Professor Ito and his colleagues in the medical faculty of Kyoto University that she has come all this way.

Osamu's wife is wearing a peach-coloured kimono. She totters towards Liz, knees close to her and hands clasped before her, and then, eyes lowered, she bows. Her face is too long and too aquiline to be beautiful in the west but Liz knows that here it is beautiful. She has an air of extreme fragility and yet of – no, not unbending, but bending strength. There is a little girl of four, with her hair cut straight across her forehead, and she too is wearing a kimono. There is a boy of seven, who is wearing patent-leather shoes with straps across the instep, black velveteen shorts and a red-and-black spotted bow tie. The boy has his mother's aquiline features.

Osamu continues to giggle with a mixture of embarrassment and pleasure. Liz has presents for all of them: a Pierre Cardin scarf for Noriko (presumably it is only on special occasions that she dresses in kimono); a doll for the little girl; three models of vintage cars for the boy; and for Osamu a cashmere pullover. It is difficult to tell if any of them, other than the little girl, is pleased. Perhaps the other three are burdened with that terrible Japanese problem of obligation and its return. Perhaps, as they appraise what Liz has insisted that they must unwrap, though it is not the Japanese custom to do so in front of the donor, and as they exclaim How beautiful! and How kind!, they are secretly trying to calculate: How much could this have cost? The little girl rocks her doll in her arms, peering down at it as it opens end shuts its blank, blue eyes.

Osamu explains that his wife speaks little English.

Never mind, you can translate for her.

Sukoshi, sukoshi, says Noriko – meaning Little, little.

They stand awkwardly for a while in the foyer, as though not knowing what to say or do next. Liz eventually suggests that perhaps the children would like an ice cream or some lemonade and Osamu and Noriko some coffee or tea.

But: Let us go, Osamu says.

He then addresses Noriko in Japanese, in a low, hissing voice, his head turned away from Liz. Noriko nods calmly, smiles, bows.

They will stay here, Osamu tells Liz. They will wait for us.

But wouldn't they like to come too?

It is better if we drive alone. The children may get tired or sick. My wife will take them into the garden. Have you seen the garden of the hotel?

She resists the temptation to tell him of what lies behind that exquisite *shoji* of her room. Not yet, she answers.

It is very beautiful.

In the carpark, he walks over, not to the car in which he first came to see her, but to a large, gleaming Datsun, that looks as if it had just come out of a showroom window. He fumbles with the key, as one does when unlocking a car door unfamiliar to one.

But this isn't . . . She oughtn't to have said that; she realizes her mistake even as the words emerge.

He flushes: My car has broken down. It is always breaking down – I told you it was old! And so I have borrowed this car from – from a friend.

This, of course, is not true. He has hired it, because he feels that for her, a foreigner and a famous doctor, a guest of the university, to travel in that beat-up old car of his would cause a terrible loss of face: for her and so for him and perhaps even for the university, if anyone were to see her in it and recognize who she was.

It's a super car.

She gets in. How much can he have paid for it? His salary cannot be large. But it would make things worse to offer to pay a half share herself.

We shall go to the house. A statement, not a question.

The house is the house in which she and Tom and the three children and this businessman, who was once simultaneously their houseboy and a student, all used to live. Muriel also used to live there but somehow Liz tends to forget that. The house stood in a fashionable suburb of the city; but because of the construction of a ring road through it and the destruction of some of the older mansions to make way for apartment blocks, it is no longer fashionable.

They drive slowly and the only words they utter is when one or the other of them points to some once familiar landmark.

What happened to the Servite Mission? Liz asks.

It has moved. Too big a house, too little money.

Oh, look, there's that bar where we used to eat that awful spaghetti when I was too lazy to cook!

It is now a very expensive restaurant. Western style.

Well, that spaghetti certainly wasn't western style, was it?

Do you remember the bath house? Osamu points.

Late at night, as she sat reading a book in the sitting-room or lay beside Tom in the bedroom, she would hear the clatter of the Japanese boy's *geta* as he returned up the road from the bath.

And the dog pound? Now it is Liz who points.

Osamu went to the pound and found their labrador there. He never liked dogs but the children had been fretful all day because of its loss.

They begin to drive down the road leading to the house. It seems narrower, dustier, and more untidy than she remembers it, and the trees seem much taller. The wooden fence round the house was solid and high. Now it dips crazily in places and at one corner there is a hole in it, which has been plugged with a ball of rusty barbed wire. Liz begins to feel slightly sick and slightly frightened. She has seen over one of those dips that the garden is a wilderness. It is as if all that work that she and Tom and Osamu put into it must have been an illusion – like those dreams she sometimes has of working out intricate formulae, unrecallable when she wakes.

Osamu stops the car and she suddenly notices that he has about him a breathy excitement, as though he had reached the top of some peak and the air were too strong for him. He gets out and then he opens the door for her and reluctantly, her face ashen and pinched, she descends. He takes her arm, but only lightly, in order to guide her over the unevennesses of the road and then up the unevennesses of the broken steps. There are a number of bells, instead of the single brass one that Osamu used to polish with so much care and pride, and these bells are all of different shapes and sizes, with name plates beside them, some in western etters and some in Japanese characters. He hesitates and then, just as she is saying Do we want to go in?, he presses one of the bells. Miss McCready, he says. But she has already seen the name, the only neatly written one among them.

Miss McCready opens the door, using her left hand while her right arm, perpetually trembling, is pressed into her side. There has been a sound of shuffling before she has appeared and Liz, being a doctor, knows that that is what is called festination and that Miss McCready is probably in the first stages of Parkinson's disease. The old woman scowls at Liz, still incapable of believing that that scatty Englishwoman who was always late for something or forgetting something at the Baptist Hospital, is now famous. Miss McCready was matron at the Baptist Hospital, where she had more power than any doctor; but now she has retired – though she still sometimes goes up there to 'help out', as she puts it, or to 'interfere', as the nurses put it.

Oh, my! she cries out, and her left hand flies to her mouth. Liz had never heard any other American woman say Oh, my! except in the cinema and here is Miss McCready, with her high colour and her high bosom, and her high hair-do, a ziggurat of greying plaits, saying it again, after all these years.

Osamu explains that Mrs Butler would like to see her old home and Miss McCready says, Well, she's very welcome to see my part of it! though there is no welcome in her tone. A tabby cat, long-backed and bushy, has now whisked out from the door behind her and stares at Liz with what seems to be an equal lack of welcome.

Liz wants to tell her, Oh, please don't bother, I'd rather remember it as I knew it, but Osamu is nodding to her to go in and Miss McCready is already shuffling off, with the cat rubbing itself against her calves as it zigzags behind her.

The house was huge and rambling, part Japanese and part western in style. A Japanese psychiatrist built it in the thirties, living in part of it and keeping his patients in the rest. It should have been an unhappy house, since it must have contained much unhappiness; even the psychiatrist had been lost at Guam, leaving behind a wife who later killed herself and an embittered mother, who was their landlady and obviously loathed them. But now, with curtains and plywood doors marking off the territories of the various tenants, it seems strangely shrunken.

This was once their sitting-room – an airy, uncluttered Japanese-style room, where they would force their awkward western guests to squat by the open windows in the summer or around a charcoal brazier in the winter. But the *shoji* have now gone from the windows and in their place are modern aluminium frames and glass; and a one-bar electric fire has superseded the brazier. There is a room divider, with a few books and old copies of the *Reader's Digest* and *Time* magazine on its shelves, along with a clutter of Japanese dolls and old postcards, propped up at random, and pottery of no value. On this side of the divider there is a bed, which also serves during the day as a divan, a crocheted rug thrown over it; two armchairs, sagging in the middle; a black-and-white television set. On the other side, there is a sink and a cooker and a pedal bin and some shelves with pots and pans and stores on them. Miss McCready was excessively tidy and clean. Miss McCready now lives in a mess of cat's hair and cat's smell, dust, worn linoleum, and a bed obviously unmade under its crocheted cover.

A panic seizes Liz as she looks around her. She is surrounded by fragments – the *tokonoma* still remains and, yes, that little window beside it does not have an aluminium frame like the rest – but she cannot get the fragments to fit. It is as though a precious cup had been smashed and she held certain of its jagged pieces in her hand but not all of them, and then tried to re-create, not the cup – that was impossible – but just her memory of it.

Miss McCready grudgingly offers some Nescafé but Liz, unable to speak, shakes her head. Miss McCready then suggests that she might ask some of the other occupants if they would mind if Liz looked over their apartments and bed-sitting-rooms; but Liz shakes her head at that too. The garden, yes, the garden – that is really what she would like to see.

Oh, the garden . . . Miss McCready sighs. Well, you know how it is? If everyone is responsible, then no one is responsible.

She can no longer do anything about it herself – she just isn't up to it any longer – and, since that nice French student left, well, the place has just gone to rack and ruin. Jimmy prefers it like that, of course, it's his jungle now, but still – she shakes her head, so that it seems to tremble in precise time to her hand – it's sad, really sad. It has taken Liz some time to realize that Jimmy is the cat.

Eventually Osamu and Liz go out into the garden, while Miss McCready, Jimmy held under her chin with her left hand, while the right arm goes on trembling, watches them balefully. She never liked Liz, never trusted her, schemed against her and gossiped about her. Oh, she always had a good conceit of herself, that one, and no doubt has an even better one now!

Osamu and Liz walk through the waist-high grass and brambles to the pond. They look out over it, its surface now tented with a thick, matted green, with a gaze of identical sorrow. This was how the pond had been when first they had come; but then Osamu said that he would clean it out and they would have goldfish in it and water lilies and other aquatic plants.

Tom took the children to the annual fare at the Baptist Hospital but, though Liz ought also to have gone – Miss McCready noticed her absence and remarked on it more than once – she said that it was much too hot and that in any case she had to wash her hair and mend some socks and do a number of other things. Osamu announced that he was going to clean out the pond. It was something that he had been planning to do for weeks but somehow he had never got round to it, so enervating was that long, humid summer.

Liz had washed her hair and then, leaving the mending and all the other little chores, she had settled down on the verandah with a novel and a thermos of iced lemonade; but she knew later, though not at the time, that all this had really been only a pretence and a pretext. She could not see the pond from the verandah, since it was round at one side of the house; but eventually she got up and, book in hand, she strolled under the trellis of rambler roses and over the yellowing lawn, until there she found him, thigh-deep in the pond. He was hacking and tugging at its vegetation with an extraordinary savagery, his hand raising a billhook and whirling it down, time and time again. His near-naked body – he was wearing only a *fundoshi* or loin cloth – was smeared with a mingling of sweat and mud, and mud even caked his eyebrows and hair.

She looked at him appraisingly and he looked up at her, the billhook raised. Neither of them smiled.

I hope there are no leeches in that water.

He laughed. Probably he did not understand what leeches meant.

How about a drink? That must be hot work.

He hesitated; then he nodded and clambered, dripping, out of the pond.

He sat on the log of a tree that they had recently had to have cut down – the centre of its trunk had contained a greenish, friable substance that disintegrated into dust in one's hand – and she went indoors to bring out a tray laden with the gin fizzes that he had now learned to like. The mud was almost dry on his squat, muscular body when she came back. He looked like some aborigine, perched there on the log.

They began to drink in silence, he still seated there and she standing; and then, when he had almost finished, she put out a hand to him, effortlessly, as she had so often dreamed of doing and thought that she would never dare to do. So easy! She put out a hand to him and he took the hand in his own mud-smeared one and she drew him to his feet and they walked like that, hands held, she always a little ahead of him, back into the house. . . .

Osamu tugs at a plant growing at the edge of the pond. It is fleshy, with a purple shine along its sharply serrated leaves, each like a miniature saw, and it resists him by slithering from his grasp time and time again. He laughs, looking down at his hands which are now covered in an evil-smelling glue. He takes a handkerchief from his pocket and wipes them.

All that work . . . And for nothing.

Well, it was beautiful for a while. Do you remember the

water lilies? She remembers the water lilies, stiff and waxen, and how he would wade among them, raking away the slime.

She has an impulse to hold out her hand to this thick-set businessman in his businessman's suit, as once she did to the muscular, near-naked student; she wonders how he would react. But then they both stroll, separate from each other, back towards the house.

Miss McCready gives them a baleful stare, as she stands on the verandah, her left hand shielding her small, extremely blue eyes.

It's so sad about that pond, Liz says.

It's so sad about the whole garden. But I'm beyond it. Seventy-six last birthday. And that Belgian slug upstairs – Miss McCready raises her voice, instead of lowering it, as she looks up to the balcony above her – knows of no exercise other than lifting a beer mug to his lips.

They go back into what was once the sitting-room. Osamu and Liz lay there, the *tatami* matting smeared with mud and Liz smeared with mud, until, suddenly, in terror, they heard footsteps above them. Mildred, whom they had supposed still to be out, must have come home earlier than expected. Then Osamu ran to his room and Liz ran to the bathroom. What's all this mud doing here? one of the children eventually asked; and Liz then explained how the labrador had leapt into the pond with Osamu and must have brought it in.

You must find it strange to return after all these years, Miss McCready says.

Very strange.

You haven't changed. It is clear that she feels that people ought to change. Especially Liz.

Haven't I? I feel that I have.

In the car, before he starts up the engine, Osamu takes some paper tissues out of the back pocket of his trousers and again carefully wipes whatever is left of the greenish stickiness of the pond plant off his hands. Then he presses the starter. Interesting, he says.

Sad.

Liz can feel the tears, unshed but waiting, pricking at the corners of her eyes. She turns her head away from him.

While Noriko prepares the lunch in the apartment, Osamu and Liz go out for a walk with the children. Osamu is reluctant for the children to come and Noriko, speaking in a low voice to him while her eyes gaze at Liz with a gentle sweetness, seems to share that reluctance. But the children are insistent, the little girl even setting up a low keening when it looks for a moment as though her brother will be taken but she will be left behind.

Oh, do let both of them come. Why not? Liz intervenes.

Do you really want them to come? Osamu finds it difficult to believe this.

Of course.

She and Osamu walked this path once before with some children, but then they were hers, not his, and it was night. Tom was away in Tokyo, standing in for an American doctor on furlough, and because it was so hot and humid in the Kyoto house, they had decided to go out and see the cormorant-fishing on the river at Arashiyama. The forest was thick on either side of them, so that it was difficult to tell how much of the fatigue that all of them felt was due to its pressure and how much to the pressure of the atmosphere.

Now it is all changed; there is no path and no forest attempting to obliterate it. Instead, there is a paved alley between the block of apartments from which they have come and the other nine making up the complex belonging to the firm for which Osamu is working. Liz feels a desolating sense of loss. It's all so different, she says. I can hardly recognize it.

Osamu stoops and picks up the little girl, who is already wailing that she can't keep up with them. Japan is changing, he answers. He is proud of a change that makes it no longer necessary for students like himself to do menial jobs for foreigners like Liz and Tom in order to make their way through college.

The little boy edges towards Liz and then, suddenly, to her amazement, she feels his hand in hers. It is a curiously rough, cold little hand, with nails that, though scrupulously clean, would be thought in need of cutting back in England. It might almost be the claw of a bird. She smiles down at him but he turns his head away, as though fearful of smiling back at her.

Well, the river is the same, with a leaden haze over the forest on either side of it and a few bathers in its waters. On either bank there are still bamboo rectangles raised up on stilts, canopies of straw above them, where people squat for refreshments; there are still omnibuses, with neatly groomed girls in uniforms officiously blowing whistles to summon errant passengers; there is still that sense of barely checked, menacing wildness – as though suddenly a typhoon might snap off the tops of the trees, a tidal wave might submerge the pleasure craft, or a volcano might erupt from one of the mountain peaks.

They hired a boat, because at that period it cost only a few shillings to do so. Night had fallen and all over the vast expanse of the river there were other boats, their cormorants, perched on their prows, silhouetted, like sinister heraldic emblems, by the braziers flaring beside them. The children were delighted; Adrienne even wanted to stroke one of the birds but Osamu told her not to, the bird might attack her. Each bird had what looked like a collar round its neck and Osamu explained that this was a device to prevent it from swallowing any fish that it caught. All this is only for tourists, he said. The men do not make money from the sale of the fish but from the hire of the boats. The oars creaked, the birds emitted a guttural sound that seemed to be a distorted echo of that creaking. One of the three men in charge of their boat banged with an oar on its side.

Suddenly Osamu, realizing that the children were totally absorbed in the spectacle of the chained, gagged birds diving for fish, turned to her: Why cannot I come to England?

Oh, Osamu! Why! We want you to come, of course we want you to come, but what sort of life would you have over there? You don't want to be a houseboy for the rest of your days – even

if we could afford to employ you. Tom's right. It's much better
for you to take this job with this pharmaceutical company that
he's found for you. You don't want to cut adrift from your
family and – and your whole *life* out here in Japan. It would be
hopeless.

She, too, was hopeless. In eleven days they would board the
P & O liner in Kobe and she would probably never see him
again.

Osamu sighed. She took his hand in hers but quickly he
withdrew it. One of the children let out a squeal. Rockets were
whizzing up into the leaden sky and then falling, in innumerable
torrents of green, red and gold over the river and the forests on
either side of it and even the mountains beyond.

They are standing on the precise spot where they disem-
barked from the boat under that continuing rain of coloured
fire. Liz wonders if Osamu remembers. The boy lets go of Liz's
hand, which has been sweating from the contact though his has
remained strangely dry, and runs down to the water's edge. He
kneels and stares at something – it looks like no more than an
upturned tin – in the shallows. Osamu, seeing what he is doing,
shouts something angry and the boy gets up. He is dirtying his
beautifully washed, beautifully pressed shorts and his long
stockings.

They're such gorgeous children, Liz says.

He clearly does not like her saying that. Perhaps, like many
Japanese, he is superstitious and fears that some malign fate may
exact retribution. He looks at his multifunctional digital watch
and tells her that it is time they went back, since Noriko said
that the meal would be ready at half past one.

The children, hers not his, ran ahead of them, half-excited and
half-fearful, up the path that wavered through the forest crowding in on either side of it. Snakes, monkeys, wild dogs, wild cats!
Or ghosts! They had been told by Osamu that you could always
recognize a Japanese ghost because it had no feet. To frighten
themselves like this only intensified the memory of the pleasure
of watching those strange, cruel-beaked birds dive for fish and

then, so unexpectedly, that downpour of fire all around them. Liz turned to Osamu and put her hands on his shoulders. No one behind, no one in front. A miracle in Japan! She kissed him, holding him close to her, as though she were the man, confident and strong, and he the woman, shrinking and pliable.

Osamu lifts up the little girl, who has been wailing fretfully. She smiles at him, the tears still on her cheeks, puts out a hand and tugs at a lock of his hair. He does not mind, because when a child is young it can do what it wishes in Japan. It is only when it is older that it must learn self-control and circumspection.

The table is laid as it might be in the west, with knives and forks and spoons and a cruet stand and white napkins fringed with lace. There are flowers on it and chairs around it. Osamu explains that Noriko has been taking lessons in western cookery. Liz wonders if she has been taking these lessons against the coming of this Englishwoman who once employed and loved her husband.

There are lamb chops, which are pinkish at the centre because they have not been cooked long enough, and potatoes that have been cooked so long that they have been reduced to a watery flour. There is a bottle of acid red wine, which, Liz notices, Osamu does not offer to Noriko. Later, there is a lemon chiffon pie, the top of which tastes as if it were indeed made of chiffon. But all this does not matter. With a mingling of pain and tranquil consoling pleasure, Liz realizes that Osamu and Noriko are totally happy with each other. Noriko may complain laughingly that her husband is always coming home late, because he has to stay up so many nights playing mahjongg with prospective customers – whom he must usually allow to win. Osamu may complain that, though Noriko has a degree from Doshisha Women's College in history, she prefers to look after the house and children than to get a job. But they are only teasing each other, there is no acrimony in all this, neither wants the other any different – in the way that Liz and Tom so often want each other different. Liz now feels that, though she is sitting so close to Osamu and though the little girl is sitting between Osamu and

Noriko, yet the husband and wife are somehow merging into each other, even as she looks at them and listens to them. Their bodies are coalescing, their faces are becoming superimposed on each other. She wonders if anyone has ever felt the same thing about herself and Tom. Perhaps Osamu did, so many years ago. It is all so different now.

They drink coffee out of thimble-like cups of Kutani china. Liz has never liked modern Kutani china, usually so bright and over-decorated; but she feels no inclination to find fault with it this afternoon, any more than with the sports pennants hanging on either side of the door (Osamu played football for Kyoto University), the two garish dolls, one male and one female, each imprisoned in a cell of glass on either end of the mantelpiece, or the view of the Houses of Parliament – in fact a dishcloth once sent by her as the kind of present that can easily be parcelled – which has been carefully pinned above the upright piano.

It is at this piano that the little boy, in his black patent-leather shoes and his spotted bow tie, now seats himself at his father's bidding. There is a hush, the little boy is nervous. Then, as he strikes the keys, legs dangling several inches from the floor, Liz realizes that what he is playing, with several wrong notes, is 'God Save the Queen'. When that is over and she has congratulated him and Osamu has patted his square, closely cropped head and Noriko has kissed him on the cheek, Liz knows, as one always knows in Japan, even though no word has been said, that it is time for her to go.

Noriko and the children accompany her and Osamu down into the courtyard, where the car is parked. Noriko is going to bow her farewell, but on an impulse Liz goes forward and kisses the Japanese woman, an arm thrown around her shoulder. The Japanese woman is plainly surprised but she is also pleased. Liz wonders if Osamu has ever spoken about their love affair in that distant past. She doubts it. But the Japanese can convey and intuit so much without any words and Liz knows that Noriko knows and, more important, feels no resentment.

You have such a happy family, Liz says as the car begins the journey along the broad, blaring highway to Kyoto.

Yes. We are happy. He says it simply. A fact.

It was right that you didn't come to England with us. *We* were right – Tom and I. Though I wanted you to come.

But Osamu makes no answer to that. Perhaps he has genuinely forgotten that he ever begged them to take him; perhaps it is less embarrassing to pretend that he has forgotten. I wish to see England, he says. One day.

Oh, do come and stay with us! We'd love that.

Of course. Thank you. I think that in maybe five years my firm will send me.

Yes, it has all been mapped out for him, as for every other employee of the company. They all know how many years it will be before, on some pretext or another, they are dispatched to the west.

I *have* enjoyed this day!

I am sorry that Tom-san could not come with you.

Yes, he so much wanted to come. But they'd only pay my fare, not his. And it's now become so expensive out here in Japan. Unbelievable!

Do you remember when we could stay for one thousand yen in a Japanese inn?

Yes! With breakfast and dinner included. That used to be – oh, about a pound.

Tom said that Osamu had better drive her and the children to Amano-Hashidate and he would follow in the train the following day. Otherwise they might be charged for the unused rooms. There were three of these rooms, divided from each other by *fusuma* that could be pulled back, fragile on their grooves, to make a single room, beautiful in all its proportions, that looked out over still, smoky expanses of water, divided by a causeway. The first room, which was large, was for Tom and Liz; the next, which was larger, was for the children; and the small one, little more than a vestibule, was for Osamu. When they arrived and

B

Liz saw the tiny room, she said, Oh, I do hope this is big enough
for you, and Osamu, surprised, replied that it was a four-and-a-
half-mat room and that, when he was a schoolboy, he had
shared just such a room with his younger brother.

That night she went to him, tiptoeing through the room in
which the three children slept, with the moonlight powdering
their upturned faces with a grey, luminous dust. She slipped off
her kimono, as, from the floor, he held out his hands to her. But,
just as she was about to kneel down on the *futon*, she saw what
looked like a ravelled piece of black string on the whiteness of
the pillow. Her hands went to her mouth when the string
suddenly wriggled. She pointed.

Osamu leapt up, naked, from the *futon*, seized one of the
transparent, plastic slippers provided by the inn, and began to
hit out wildly. It was a *mukade*, he said, and Liz knew that that
meant a kind of poisonous centipede, though until now she had
never seen one. Long after the insect was no more than pulp on
the *tatami*, he went on beating at it, as she had seen Japanese
women, their faces flushed with a kind of obsessive malevolence,
pound away at rice in a pestle, in order to reduce it to a pulp for
rice-balls.

There was a wail from the next-door room. He had woken
one of the children. Liz slipped back into her kimono, slid the
fusuma open and whispered: It's nothing, go back to sleep, don't
worry. Then she whispered to Osamu that it was all too difficult,
every sound could be heard, she must return to her room. The
sight of that naked figure slashing out at the insect with flushed
face and flailing arm, had filled her with more dread than the
wail of the child. Yet a *mukade*, it was well known, could cause
death with its sting, and it was natural enough that Osamu
should have been so violent.

What happened to Mrs Budden? Osamu suddenly asks. He
means Mildred.

Liz explains that she has lost touch with her, letters have not
been answered, perhaps – who knows? – she may be dead. She
went back to Canada to live with a sister and, after all, she was

no longer young even in those far-off times when she occupied the two top-floor rooms as a lodger.

Liz wonders why he should suddenly ask about her. Except that he was always convinced, however much Liz herself might pooh-pooh the idea, that Mildred knew about them. She watched, she listened: he was sure of that.

Osamu laughs: Direct Method, he says.

Yes. She believed in the Direct Method.

They reach the hotel and they are now going to say goodbye. They will not see each other again for – well, all those years that will elapse before Osamu's service to the company is rewarded with a visit to England. He puts his hand in his pocket and he takes out a small, beautifully wrapped package.

A souvenir, he says.

What is it? I know I shouldn't open it now but may I break all the Japanese rules and do so?

He nods, smiling.

She sits down on a chair in the foyer and, her fingers trembling and clumsy, first unties the ribbon and then peels off first the layer of wrapping paper and then the tissue paper beneath it.

I remember that you collect them.

It is a Chinese snuff bottle, carved out of tourmaline in a pattern of water lilies. As she looks at it, she thinks of the pond and of the near-naked figure emerging from it, daubed with mud, with the fleshy pink-and-green lilies opening their mouths around him.

She and Tom no longer collect snuff bottles, because soon after their return from Japan they were so short of money that they had to auction off their whole collection. But she does not tell Osamu this, of course, as she begins carefully to rewrap the bottle first in its tissue paper and then in its wrapping paper and to retie the ribbon around it.

Tom will love it, she says. How kind you are!

No obligation now weighs on him: not for the Pierre Cardin scarf, not for the cashmere pullover, not for the doll, not for the three model vintage cars, not even for the hours – so few! – that

she lay with him. This is a museum piece and he has paid it all
off, the whole debt. She can understand why, though they are
about to say goodbye, he has the air of a man who has just
emerged from a law court, unexpectedly acquitted.

Dear Osamu . . .

Well . . .

He gives that embarrassed giggle. Then he says that he must
get home, he is sure that she has many, many things to do, he
hopes that she will enjoy the rest of her trip and that she will
come back soon to Japan. She planned to ask him up to her
room but now she knows that it would be humiliatingly pointless
to do so.

The lift-boy glances down at the package in her hand, no
doubt wondering what this grey-haired foreign woman has
bought or what she has been given. The package feels extraordinarily heavy to Liz, as though it were some huge stone that she
had balanced in her palm.

She goes into her room and she puts down that terrible weight
and then she goes over to that blond frame of wood covered with
nacreous paper. She stares at the notice: PLEASE DO NOT
OPEN.

This is a room. What is it?

It is a prison.

No. This is a room. Repeat.

It is a prison.

No, no. Let me give you the Japanese equivalent. This is a
room – *Sore wa zashiki desu.*

Indirect Method.

She was about to force the *shoji* apart again but now she
leaves it.

The Wake

FOR SO many years Frosso had been there, head held high and bosom thrust out, on the invisible escalator a few steps above me. Then, as if the section on which she had been standing had all at once speeded up with an existence of its own, she had plunged over the top and vanished from my sight. But, mysteriously, the people who had been clustered all around her, parasitic fungi on the sturdy tree of her life – 'the little circle' she called them – had not vanished with her.

Frosso had been one of the greatest of the *bouzouki* singers of her day, no Greek would dispute that; and even when her voice had grown ragged and rough, its gears stripped from her reckless exploitation of its phenomenal range, when her chain-smoking had induced a chronic bronchitis, when the crudely applied make-up could no longer conceal the deep grooves from nose to chin and when her voracity for food and drink had made her body dumpy and lumpy, she never lost her public. I had first known her in the days, soon after the war, when she performed in a garishly lit taverna on the straight, long road, Odos Syngrou, that bumped from Athens to Phaleron. In her coarse gipsy way, all jangling jewellery, tumbling jet-black hair and flashing satins and sequins, she had been a beauty then; and her voice, for all its nasal stridency, was also a beauty. She sang for the most part of thwarted love, separation and sudden death, on a rickety wooden platform under brilliant stars to an audience of soldiers, sailors, airmen, labourers, small shop-keepers, artisans, whores and a scattering of foreigners like myself. The nights were hot and she sweated freely, the glistening fabric of her dress darkening under the armpits and about her midriff.

Later I learned, both from her and from members of 'the little circle', of her forced marriage, a village orphan of fifteen, to a man, part huckster and part gangster, of over sixty. She had run away from him and there had been a period, of which she had never made any pretence, in a brothel in Piraeus. She had married again, a weakly youth from an impoverished family of Greeks from Asia Minor, and she had had her only child, a son, by him. The youth had died in the war, unpredictably heroic but predictably ineffectual, trying to place a bomb under the car of a German general but succeeding only in blowing up himself. Somehow Frosso, hunted by the Gestapo, had managed to escape to Egypt, abandoning her son with her dead husband's sister; and it was there, in Alexandria, that she had first begun to win her fame, singing to Greek servicemen marooned in an exile as desolate as her own.

In the later years of prosperity the road from Athens to Phaleron was widened and smoothed and, instead of being lit, as once, by irregular splashes of ochre light, it was now illuminated uniformly and brightly from one end to the other. The once bare wood of the tables was decently draped in linen. There were menus, so cumbersome that it was difficult to handle them, tinny vases of flowers, waiters in greasy dinner-jackets, American cars and German tourist buses and Japanese motorcycles ridden by boys in Gucci shoes accompanied by girls in Pucci head-scarves. The soldiers, sailors, airmen, labourers, small shop-keepers and artisans either vanished or could be seen in shadowy groups standing beyond the tables. The whores no longer looked like whores. But Frosso changed little. The jewellery that she now wore was real but it still looked as though she had fished it up off a stall in a village market. Her clothes came from Paris or Florence or London but, on that sturdy peasant body, they still had the air of having been run up by some local dress-maker, her eyes sore from sewing on all those sequins and fringes and feathers. Visiting her once in hospital ('My plumbing has never really worked properly since that old rogue in Patras did that job on me') I was shocked to see that her once luxuriant black hair had gone thin and grey. By then I had grown so used to a variety of extravagant wigs – ebony, auburn, brown, henna-red, blond, even platinum – that I regarded them as being as much an integral part of her as the caps on her formerly irregular teeth or the falsies beneath her brassières.

She had had a cold, she had been tired. Returning from a series of concerts abroad, she had gone to the television studios early the following morning and had worked all day and late into the evening on a programme for New Year's Eve. I had expected her to dine with me but she had telephoned, more than an hour after she was due, to say, 'Darling, don't be cross, please don't be cross, but I just can't make it. I'm done in – dead! I'm fit for nothing. Eleni will have to lay me out.' Eleni had worked with her in that Piraeus brothel and had worked for her, except when they had one of their frequent rows, ever since. 'Oh, Frosso, really!' I said, not believing her for a moment. 'Who is it this time?' 'No, really, darling! I know that I'm not always entirely truthful but this time there's no one and nothing else at all. Honest!' I still did not believe her. But she went home, as she had said that she was going to do, had a bath and, after drinking a glass of neat whisky, got into her bed and died. As simple as that. All her actions were simple. There was a post-mortem, because 'the little circle' insisted, with morbid relish, that she must have killed herself. Everyone knew, they said, that her affair with that Dimopoulos boy had blown itself out in a tempest of mutual recriminations; that she had been bitterly disappointed and hurt that another Greek singer, a mere girl with hardly any reputation, had been chosen instead of her for a television series by the BBC; that she had been in debt ever since her manager had given her some ruinous advice about investments. . . . But, not for the first time, 'the little circle' had totally misjudged her. Frosso had had a fatal heart-attack.

No one close to me has ever caused me so much exasperation; and now, as so often before, I felt exasperation as well as grief at the suddenness of her going. She had so often telephoned to tell me, at the last moment, that she could not make a date; and when

I had asked why, had then explained that she would be in Cairo or Istanbul or New York. Now she would be somewhere even more remote; and she would not return. Having received the news, I sat on a rented sofa and stared at the rented table before me. There was a scratch across the surface of the table and suddenly I remembered how, many months before, Frosso had put her legs up and made that scratch with the heel of a boot of red Russian leather. Inadvertently she was always inflicting such wounds on the objects around her – wine on tablecloths, lipstick on towels, mud on carpets, chips on cups; and inadvertently she was also always inflicting wounds on those closest to her. I went on staring at that diagonal scratch across the table. At that moment I seemed to feel it, jagged and raw, like a scratch across the retinas of my eyes.

Our nickname for Frosso's son had always been 'Portfolio' for as long as I could remember. Wherever he went at whatever hour of the day, he carried what he called 'My portfolio' with him. This was a black leather briefcase with his initials in gold on its flap. In restaurants he would prop it against a table leg, place it on an empty chair beside him or even cradle it uncomfortably in his lap. He took it to the theatre or cinema, to dinner parties, on boat trips and car trips, even to the beach. He never opened it to remove anything or to put anything in it. What did it contain? Jokingly, the little circle would speculate. Drugs? Obscene photographs? Money that he feared to entrust to a bank? Sometimes one of us would ask him, to receive the reply: 'Papers, just papers.' He worked in the office of an estate agent and I used to imagine crumpled, dog-eared 'particulars' of 'desirable properties' in Glyphada, Vouliagmeni or Varkisa.

He was a grey man. Grey face, grey suits, grey hair. Narrow-shouldered, shallow-chested, with the thin, soft, spatulate fingers that so often go with debility of physique or character. Voice clipped, often barely audible; speech pedantic in its elaborate periphrases and its tendency to prefer a *katherevousa* word to a demotic one. Frosso's attitude to him always struck me as similar

to that of a dog-owner who is not also a dog-lover to her pet.
Feed him regularly, deworm and deflea him regularly, give him
his regular exercise and a warm place to sleep. If his nose is dry
or he loses his appetite, take him to the vet. The poor mutt, never
having been owned by anyone else, can see no difference: that's
how all dog-owners must treat their dogs. He is attached to her,
wagging his tail when she returns home and putting it between
his legs when she leaves it.

Mimi had never married. For many years there had been a
woman, spinster daughter of a retired major with whom she lived
in a hideous, stuffy little flat in the outer suburbs. Mimi had
visited her once a week and once a week he had taken her out to
the theatre, the cinema or just a café for a cup of tea or coffee and
a sickly cake. Then the major had died, the woman had come into
some money; and shortly afterwards she had surprised everyone
by marrying an elderly American teacher of English and leaving
with him for Salonica or Patras or Halkis, where he was to take
up a new post. 'Mimi is so upset,' Frosso said; but Mimi really
did not care.

Curiously, since a dog usually cares about the loss of his
mistress, he did not even seem to care greatly about his mother's
abrupt departure. When I offered my condolences, he cleared his
throat, shifted the briefcase from one hand to the other and said
'Yes. Well. Thank you.' Then he added: 'If she had to go, it was
the best way, wasn't it?' This conversation took place in the
doorway of Frosso's flat. He did not ask me in. Perhaps he had
been about to go out; perhaps he just did not want to prolong
the conversation. He was wearing a black tie, its knot pinched
tight, and a black arm band, no doubt stitched there by Eleni, on
the sleeve of his jacket. I wanted to see Eleni, I wondered what
would now happen to her, so fat, so foolish, so capricious. She
would miss those screaming matches and even more she would
miss the pleasure of shaking her head over Frosso's extrava-
gances and follies.

'I'll be at the funeral, of course,' I said.

'It'll be very modest.'

He sounded as though he wanted to exclude me. But he could not do that, any more than he could exclude Frosso's public.

There were hundreds, yes, literally hundreds, of people crowded into the cemetery. There were newspaper photographers perched, like giant birds, on the marble mausolea. There were television cameramen, noisily peremptory. There was a small man with a large tape-recorder strapped to him, who kept approaching this or that famous actor, singer or politician with his microphone. The winter sun glittered on the long petrified locks of a young girl whose head was lowered over the keys of a stone grand piano, her uptilted nose freckled with moss; on the bald pate, spattered with bird lime, of an eminent politician, who, one arm inserted in the front of his morning-coat, looked as if he were being frustrated for all eternity from scratching himself under an armpit; on the high cheekbones of an elderly matron encased in a lacy nightdress of marble as she lay out with a giant scroll for her bolster. Heels crunched gravel or sank into oozing grass. The taller angled their necks like antennae; the shorter stood on tiptoe with occasional ineffectual little jumps. A low hum, as of bees about to quit their hive, was intermittently overlaid by a sob, a wail or a rasping exclamation of protest ('Please!' 'My foot!' 'Do you mind!' 'Your umbrella!') The bushy-bearded priest, intoning dramatically through his beaky nose, stopped from time to time, fiercely frowning, to remind everyone that this was a religious ceremony. But, silenced for a moment, the hubbub then continued. Mimi stood, totally still, his head bowed, beside the priest, with a slightly smirking expression. Needless to say, he was holding the 'portfolio' before him in both his hands, rather as though he were using it to shield his genitals.

When the first earth pattered down on the coffin, there was a piercing scream from Eleni, who struggled forward from behind the priest, her black hat, with its bee-keeper's veil, all askew and mascara smudged like a bruise over a cheekbone, while hands, male and female, attempted to restrain her. Plumper and paler than I had ever seen her before, her scarlet-rimmed mouth a cavern of anguish, she fell on one knee, the gravel ripping a black stocking and grazing the knee beneath it. The chattering ceased, the wailing and sobbing rose to a crescendo. Only Mimi still remained totally unmoved, absently raising one of the hands that were gripping the 'portfolio' to brush away a fallen leaf from the shoulder of his coat. Minor actresses threw themselves about in paroxysms of grief as though auditioning for major roles. A banker, who had briefly been Frosso's lover until his stinginess had made her abandon him, blew a valedictory bugle call into a handkerchief the size of a head scarf. A man equally imposing, one of her creditors, bellowed out 'Frosso! Frosso! Frosso!' as though imploring her to climb back out of the grave and write him a cheque.

As, at last, everyone began to trail away down the hill from the cemetery, Eleni touched my arm. Her hat, with its bee-keeper's veil, was still askew, there was still the bruise of mascara on the cheekbone and she – or someone else – had tied a handker-chief around her knee. But her face now had the cheerfully sated expression of someone who has broken a protracted fast with a good guzzle. 'You'll come back to the apartment, won't you?' When I looked doubtful, she went on in a whisper; 'Mimi wants it. Not everyone. Just the little circle.' I had never cared to think of myself as one of the little circle, living off and on and through Frosso, but it was impossible to refuse. I nodded. Eleni at once slipped a black-gloved hand under my arm, in exactly the same way as Frosso used to do when we were walking together. It was the first time that Eleni had ever touched me.

The little circle sat in a little circle. Spindly gold-lacquered tables supported French hand-painted thimbles of muddy coffee and Casa Pupo-type plates, each shaped and coloured like a lettuce leaf, with a tiny cake and a curious implement, a fork with two of its three prongs welded together, resting on it. Frosso's taste had always been awful.

'So many people.'

'She would have liked that.' (Yes, she was used to full houses.)

'A beautiful voice, the priest's.' (His brother was a famous actor.)

'So many flowers.'

'I don't think I've ever seen so many flowers at a funeral.'

'Frosso always loved flowers.' (Often, even in the depths of winter, she would stop at the stalls opposite the Grande Bretagne Hotel when we had emerged from the bar or the restaurant, and extravagantly buy bunch after bunch, piling them into my arms and then having the assistant pile them into her own.)

'Was Prevelakis there?'

'Yes. I saw him. And Kondoulis too.'

'Everyone was there.' (Frosso always invited her former lovers to her parties.)

'These éclairs are delicious.'

'I know I shouldn't but I just can't resist . . .'

'They must be from Floka.' (Frosso would sit out on the pavement outside Floka, the charms on her gold bracelet jangling as she stretched out to take yet another cake.)

'Where is Mimi?'

But Mimi was there, seated in a straight-backed chair, the 'portfolio' at his feet, just a brief distance beyond the little circle. That was how he had always been; and he had always gone unnoticed, then as now.

'You'll miss her, Mimi.'

'We'll all miss her.'

'But Mimi more than anyone.'

Mimi said nothing. His bony knees and his bony ankles touched each other. His bony hands lay in his lap, nervelessly resting one on top of the other. His collar looked too tight for his long, slender neck. There was again that faintly smirking expression on his grey anonymous face.

Everyone seemed to be waiting for something; and suddenly I knew what it was. We had so often sat like this, making trivial, stilted, bored conversation to each other while waiting for Frosso. She had invited us to tea, to drinks or to dinner and she was either late or had forgotten. Or else, a performance over,

she was having a bath and changing into 'something comfortable'. Odours from that bath, crudely insistent, would creep
down the passageway lined with garish watercolours of the
islands, the work of an untalented French protégé, briefly
Frosso's lover, and seep into the sitting-room. The 'something
comfortable' would be soft and loose and long and feathery.
'Well, my children!' She would go to the drinks cupboard and
the ouzo, which she always preferred to the more fashionable
and expensive gin, vodka or whisky, would gurgle into a
tumbler. 'How was I?' It was always 'How was I?' after a
performance, never 'How are you?' She would kiss this member
of the little circle on the cheek and hold out a hand to be kissed
to this other.

Perhaps Mimi had been following the same train of recollection, because he now got up, elbows jutting oddly, went over to
the drinks cabinet and poured out for himself a tumbler of ouzo.

'Ice, Eleni?'

'In the bucket.'

Everyone watched him. Usually he did not drink and certainly
none of us had ever seen him drink ouzo. Opaque eddies whirled
away from the ice cubes, one, two, three. He held the glass to
his pointed chin, as though deliberating whether to drink from
it or not, his pale green, almond-shaped eyes under their high-
arched brows suddenly abstracted and dreamy. Then he returned
slowly to the straight-backed chair, the 'portfolio' still resting
against one leg.

'I wonder what will happen to the television programme.'

'Apparently she'd recorded less than half.'

'I imagine that they'll scrap it.'

'She promised me to use me in the next one.'

'She promised me.'

'She promised me.'

Frosso often broke appointments but never promises. They
all sounded vaguely affronted.

'It's hard to believe that door won't open and she won't come
through.'

'Never again.'

'Never.'

Still the little circle seemed to be waiting; and still the trivial, stilted, bored chatter went on. Eventually I got up to try to find myself a glass of something stronger than the coffee; and it was then, with surprise, that I noticed that Mimi had vanished. His glass and the 'portfolio' had vanished too. No one else seemed to be aware of his absence. Perhaps he had wearied of us. Perhaps, like a dog that only slowly realizes that his mistress has gone not for an hour but forever, he had only now come to terms with the finality of Frosso's departure. The minutes passed; he did not return.

Eventually I asked Eleni, who had been cackling flirtatiously at the jokes of an elderly *boulevardier*, 'Where is Mimi?'

She shrugged and pulled a little face. She did not care. No one cared.

Nor did anyone except myself seem to notice when an odour, crudely insistent, crept down the passageway and seeped into the living-room in which we were sitting in our little circle. Was I suffering some kind of hallucination? I gulped at my brandy.

'So many people.'

'She would have liked that.'

'A beautiful voice, the priest's.'

'So many flowers.'

Invisible fingers seemed to have lifted the arm of a gramophone and set it back on a record.

'Was Prevelakis there?'

'Yes. I saw him. Kondoulis too.'

I heard a rustle from the passageway: something soft and long and loose and feathery. The door opened. 'Well, my children!'

It was Frosso, Frosso herself, trailing yards of purple chiffon that clashed dramatically and horribly with the wig of henna-red hair that swept up from her forehead and tumbled in extravagant ringlets about her shoulders. She swayed towards the drinks cabinet, glass in hand, on high-heeled mules, the pink of which clashed, dramatically and horribly, with both négligée and wig. We all stared in amazement – one of the two minor actresses even gave a little whimper as she picked up the ouzo bottle and, charm bracelet tinkling, poured out from it. Then she turned her face, the make-up caked on it like a thick impasto, and asked: 'How was I?' The voice was improbably deep – even deeper than the one to which we had been for so long accustomed.

'Mimi!'

'*Mimi!*'

'"*Me chiamano Mimi! Non so perché*",' she sang out. Then she threw herself into an armchair with the old theatrical abandon and turned to me: 'Darling, be an angel, give me a cigarette!' Frosso usually smoked the cigarettes of others.

I produced one and, out of habit, lit it, removed it from my mouth and handed it to her. 'Thanks.' She drew deeply. 'I've been longing for one for ages.' Mimi never smoked. Red-tipped fingers ran through henna-red hair, clashing dramatically and horribly. 'Well, don't look so tragic, my dears!'

'Mimi!'

'*Mimi!*'

'For God's sake, why don't you all have some ouzo instead of all that coffee? Eleni! I can't stand all this gentility. Eleni!'

Eleni got to her feet and, like a sleep-walker, limped over to the drinks cabinet and, with shaking hands, began to get out tumblers.

'More than that! Don't be so mean! Go on!'

The bottle rattled against the rim of a glass.

'Cheers, my children!'

'Cheers!'

We all gulped, because there seemed nothing else to do. Then we either glanced furtively at each other or stared at the carpet.

'Fill up! Eleni! Where *is* the woman?'

Eleni got up from a chair behind the sofa and limped over to the ouzo bottle.

'Come on! Let's get really pissed, my children!'

Glasses were filled to the brim and first nervously and then with growing enthusiasm were drunk.

'Eleni! Get moving!.

This time, surprisingly, Eleni answered back as she had always done to Frosso. 'Don't shout at me like that! Keep a civil tongue in your head!'

'Oh, for God's sake! If you don't like working for me, get back to that Piraeus brothel!'

Muttering under her breath, Eleni began to splash out the ouzo.

'Cheers, darlings!'

'Cheers!'

Two or three of the little circle swallowed their ouzo at a single gulp.

'Eleni!'

'You'll all be drunk!'

'That's what we want to be. Come on!'

Chiffon swished as she scrambled up out of the armchair and walked unsteadily to the hi-fi deck in one corner. She rummaged among the records; the only ones there were her own. She pulled one out of its sleeve and pushed it roughly on to the turntable. The jangling of *bouzoukia*, made even more tinny by the age of the record, clattered out from the speakers at either side of the fireplace. She staggered into the middle of the little circle, extended her arms and, swaying in time to the rhythmic throb of the music, opened her mouth and began to sing.

'*Pame sta bouzoukia* . . . Let's go to the *bouzoukia* . . .' It had been one of Frosso's old numbers, probably one of the first she ever recorded, and I remembered it from the hot nights under the stars in the taverna in Odos Syngrou. The *boulevardier* began to clap softly in time. As in those drag acts back in London, the voice, ruthlessly cutting through the blur of the instruments like a wire through cheese, seemed to come not from the two speakers but from the mouth, crudely outlined in crimson, opening and shutting before us.

'Bravo!'

'Now sing us "*Strose to stroma sou . . .*"!'

'No, no! "*Then eimai o Giorgos sou . . .*"!'

'Later, later! Now let me rest my voice a little, children.' She splashed more ouzo into a tumbler not her own and drained it at a gulp. 'Eleni! Put on a *hassapiko*! Come on! Get moving!'

Eleni fumbled among the records still muttering to herself.

'Who's going to dance with me?'

'Me!'

'Me!'

Five of them – four men dressed all in black and the dishevelled figure in the henna-red wig and the pink feathered mules – threw arms over each other's shoulders and began to stamp out the Butcher's Dance. I watched from the shadows of a corner, at once bewildered, fascinated and appalled. I was remembering how it was said that, during wakes in remote villages in Macedonia, even today the mourners would take turns to whirl round and round the peasant hovel with the corpse in their arms. Here, with a surrogate corpse, the mourners were performing the same ritual in affirmation of the life, joy and self-abandonment that Frosso had always had in such abundance. The music grew louder and louder, the dancing more and more frenetic. One mule flew off and the other was kicked away to join it. The toe-nails on the now bare feet were the same crimson as the finger-nails. The impasto of make-up was speckled with sweat. Sweat was darkening the purple chiffon under the armpits and at the midriff.

Then the clatter of music stopped.

'Bravo, Frosso! Bravo! To your health!' The little circle had all risen, laughing and shouting, to their feet. The squat, bald man whom I had recognized as Frosso's doctor picked up one of the lettuce-leaf plates and hurled it to the ground where it shattered into fragments. One of the two minor actresses followed suit but her plate bounced, unbroken, off a rug. Someone hurled another plate.

Suddenly the panting, sweating, dishevelled figure in the purple négligée raised an arm so that its crook hid the thickly daubed face from our gaze and rushed from the room. A door banged far down the corridor.

The little circle looked mutely at each other. Someone shrugged. Someone gave a nervous titter. Someone said, 'Ought we to go to see?' Someone began to pick up the fragments of broken crockery.

'*You* go,' someone said to me.

'Yes, you go. You know Mimi best of us.'

'Yes, you.'

'You.'

But none of us had ever known Mimi; the ignorance of all of us was similarly complete.

Eleni pushed me and I remember feeling a sudden mute rage against her. I all but struck her. 'Go! Go see!'

I went.

The henna-red wig lying like some dead animal beside him on Frosso's huge double bed, stripped now to suspender belt and brassière, his back to me and his face pressed into the folds of the purple négligée, Mimi was sobbing over and over again, in the voice of a distracted child: 'Mama! Mama! Mama!'

I approached; put out a hand; retreated. I trod on something, looked down and saw that it was one of the falsies.

'Mimi.'

But the insistent wailing continued: 'Mama! Mama! Mama!'

I returned to the sitting-room. 'Let's go,' I said. 'Better if we go.'

'Is he all right?'

'Are you sure?'

'What was he doing?'

'Yes,' I said. 'Yes, he's all right. He's all right.'

Silently, one by one, the little circle all trooped out of the flat, Eleni following us.

Sundays

'DID you remember to bring the Sundays, darling?'

'No, I left them on the plane.'

'Fuck!'

A few moments later a boy joined the man and the woman in the garden of the villa. 'Did Daddy remember to bring the Sundays?'

'No, Mark, your father did not remember to bring the Sundays. In spite of my reminding him on the telephone last night.'

'Oh, fuck!'

'You mustn't use that word, Mark. You know I've told you not to use that word. It's an ugly, inexpressive word that suggests a certain poverty.'

'Well, you're always going on about how poor we are.'

'I meant poverty of imagination and vocabulary.'

'I suppose I could get into the car and drive all the way back to Milan before shaving or having any breakfast or unpacking, and say to someone at the Alitalia desk, "Please could I have the Sunday papers that I left on the plane because my dear wife and my dear son seem to be unable to survive without them."'

'I hardly think that'll be necessary, though it's generous of you to offer. We'll survive.'

'You could get them in Como, Daddy. They'll probably have them in Como by now. They usually do by Monday.'

'Daddy is not going to waste a lot of petrol by going into Como. If you want them that badly, then you can go into Como yourself.'

'*I* don't want them that badly. I thought that you did.'

Mrs Newman listened to her daughter, son-in-law and grandson from the half-open window of her bedroom, as she sat before her dressing-table mirror, bunching up handful after handful of her dry wispy hair and stabbing it with the hairpins. She held two hairpins between her teeth and another rested in the soft fleece of her bedjacket, where it had fallen unregarded. Her eyes ached as though from the flash of those swords striking against each other down there in the garden, among the deckchairs and the breakfast crockery and the sleeping dogs.

'There was something I particularly wanted to see in the *Observer* supplement, Mummy. It really is too bad!'

'Well, you can't, that's all. There are at least a hundred paperbacks in the sitting-room that you can read.'

'I've read them.'

'Not all of them. Don't talk nonsense. Or, if a book is beyond your powers, how about some weeding?'

'I thought that Giovanni was supposed to do the weeding.'

'Giovanni can't do everything all the time. Even if we do pay him more than anyone else ever paid any gardener on Lake Como.'

'This coffee's cold, Ellen.'

'Well, of course it's cold, darling. We had breakfast ages ago.'

'Couldn't you make some more? Or is that asking too much?'

'Oh, do make it yourself. You can see I've settled down to sunbathe.'

'That's a nice welcome when I've flown all the way over here to be with you for less than a week.'

'Oh, Christ, I feel depressed!'

'No boy of fifteen has any right to feel depressed. At your age I didn't know the meaning of the word. Depressed! Why, you've got *everything*!'

'You've got to admit, Jack, there's something terribly lowering about this lake.'

'Then why the hell did you decide that you must have a villa here? For God's sake, surely it isn't unreasonable of me to expect some hot coffee when I arrive here all the way from London for less than a week.'

'*I* decided that I must have a villa here? I did no such thing. I said that it would be nice to have some kind of retreat in Italy. It was you who then, in your infinite wisdom, picked on this hole.'

The swords flashed on in the sunlit garden beneath her; but she looked out over them to the calm lake, iridescent scarves of mist draping its further corners and trailing over the sides of the mountains. There were three tourist buses far down there, outside the Hotel Bellevue, and if she screwed up her eyes against the low morning sun, she could see women in brightly coloured frocks and men in brightly coloured shirts and trousers clambering aboard. She remembered the clop-clop-clop of hooves up and down what had not then been a highway but a narrow winding road. She remembered the small, bow-legged hunchback, like some wizened former jockey, who sold rose-scented nougat from a funny little stall on wheels. She remembered a parasol that she had lost, forgotten on the boat most probably, its handle the head of a swan carved in ivory. She remembered the sweating, hairy men who played *boccia* on the green space beyond and behind the hotel and how they would stare at her or any of the other foreign women, their loud, angry-seeming voices (of course they were not really angry) falling away as they did so.

'You remember nothing. *Nothing.* I've only to ask you to do something for you to forget it.'

'I have more important things to remember than the Sundays. Such as earning enough money to keep you and that bone-idle son of yours in luxury in this villa. Not to mention your mother.'

'My bone-idle son – or, rather, *our* bone-idle son – has just finished a strenuous term.'

'I'll believe in that strenuous when I see his report.'

The swords continued to flash and the ache between her eyes gathered itself into a tighter and tighter knot. Mrs Newman splashed some eau-de-cologne on to a handkerchief and held it first to one and then to the other shrunken cheek. The flesh tingled comfortingly. Then she sighed, picked up her bag, picked up her stick with its rubber ferrule. She had had another, better stick, the handle of which seemed to fit itself exactly to her small, arthritic hand, but the boy had broken it while using it for some undivulged purpose – bird-nesting? nut-gathering? – in the woods above the villa.

Out in the garden she kissed her son-in-law – this stocky, blue-chinned, balding businessman whom she always felt, even after all these years, to be a stranger. At such times he always put a hand on each of her shoulders as though he were about to force her to her knees in submission to his will. His cheek tasted rough and salt on her lips.

'Daddy forgot to bring the Sundays.'

'Now, look here, I don't want to hear another fucking word about those fucking Sundays.'

'Must you use that word in front of mother?'

'It can't be the first time she's heard it in this household.'

'Where are you going, Granny?'

'For a stroll. Just for a stroll.'

'For heaven's sake, mother! Why do you want to go out for a stroll? It's going to be a scorcher. We don't need the Sundays to tell us that. Come and sit down here in the garden with us.'

'Make yourself some coffee, mother. And make me some too while you're about it, since neither this wife nor this son of mine seems disposed to do so.'

'God, what a depressing morning!'

'No woman with as little to do as you has any right to feel depressed. If you were Giovanni's wife, you would be taking in other people's washing.'

'And if I were his daughter, I'd be walking the streets of Milan. Yes, I know.'

Mrs Newman let herself out of the rusty iron gate with its enamel plate '*Attenti ai cani*', even though the two dogs did nothing but sleep and eat, and then began the slow descent down the cobbled *muletiere*. Whoever had constructed it had obviously misjudged the extent of a human pace. To go from each level to the next, it was necessary either to take a giant stride or to take one normal step followed by a child's one. Behind the high wall, trailing its wisteria (it was strange that wisteria no longer seemed to have any scent) she could hear the scrape and clash of those three swords against each other.

An old man in boots and a shiny black alpaca coat, a sack over his shoulder, was mounting towards her. He paused, a hand pressed to the small of his back, and beamed at her, revealing chipped, nicotine-stained teeth. '*Buon*' *giorno, Signora.*' His breath wheezed and whistled. Before Giovanni, it was he who had tended the garden as he had done for more than forty years; but there had been angry words, most of them unintelligible to him though he had understood their gist, and he had never come back. The family told all their neighbours that he had let them down disgracefully; but since he had been owed several thousand lire, which they had made no attempt to pay him, he might have said the same of them.

'*Buon*' *giorno, Bruno,*' Mrs Newman replied. She would have liked to have paused for a little to have a conversation with him in her execrable Italian but loyalty prevented her. 'Must you talk to that horrible old man after the way that he's behaved to us?' her daughter had once demanded viciously when she had come on the two of them exchanging a few words by the gate.

The little hydrofoil – her son-in-law had laughed at its 'thoroughly pretentious' name, *La Freccia delle Azalee*, 'The arrow of the azaleas' – was skimming across the lake. It was not really graceful but it looked graceful from here – like some swan, she thought fancifully, flying low above the water. She wondered if she would reach the quay in time, the boat must be early; and then, as she hurried on, the toe of her left shoe caught against a cobble and she fell heavily against the wall on that side. Now that she was old, she noticed that she bled easily. Where the rough stones had grazed her forearm, small beads of crimson were already beginning to swell. She held a handkerchief, drawn from the waistband of her dress, to them, her lips drawn in, in frowning concentration; and so intent was she on doing this that at first she was wholly unaware of the throbbing of her ankle. But the throbbing intensified; and as she walked on, leaning heavily now on the stick that fitted so uncomfortably to her hand, it was as if, somewhere in her ankle, two small bones were rasping against each other. I wonder if I've broken something? But if I have, surely I couldn't go on walking?

The boatman saw her hobbling down the steps and, because they were early, he decided to wait. But she did not know that and so she hobbled even faster, waving her stick to catch his attention and even calling out in her heavily accented Italian, '*Aspetta! Momento! Vengo!*'

She bought her return ticket and the boatman held out a hand to her, the palm dry and calloused, to help her along the narrow gangway. She gasped, '*Grazie! Grazie mille!*' and made her way into the stifling cabin, which was full of Italian women with baskets and children, a group of local schoolboys sprawled out over the seats and puffing ostentatiously at cigarettes even though a notice said '*Vietato fumare*', and about a dozen young German tourists in the skimpiest of clothes. She looked round for somewhere to sit and a beautiful German girl, with a skin so translucent that the sun slanting through the porthole seemed to shine through it to the perfect bones beneath, got up and pointed: '*Bitte.*' She was wearing the shortest of shorts, ragged at the ends, and a blouse that obviously had no brassière beneath it.

'Oh, no, my dear . . .' Mrs Newman said, feeling strangely breathless at the nearness of the girl's youth and health and beauty.

'Please.' This time it was said in English.

At that, Mrs Newman sat down. She let her head fall back on the greasy rest behind it, oblivious of the handkerchief, now encrusted with dried blood, that was wrapped about her forearm, of the throbbing of her ankle and of the shouts and scuffles of the schoolboys. She loved the eagerness and freshness of that girl and her companions, their solemn faces suddenly lighting up as the sun picked out now one stretch and now another of the lake, making it flash with fire. '*Schön! Wunderbar! Sehr schön!*'

Once the girl turned and smiled down at her and between them there was suddenly this strange complicity, though they had never seen each other before and probably would never see each other again. The breeze was cool on her bare arms and her throat and her forehead. She could see the Hotel Bellevue through the porthole and she remembered once again that rose-scented taste of the nougat and the sweating, hairy men with their swelling forearms, their loud shouts and laughter and the frank, almost brutal way in which they stared at any of the foreign women who passed. The three tourist buses had gone.

It was hot when she stepped off the boat, the boatman again holding out to her that dry, calloused hand. He had long, drooping moustaches and hair parted as though by an incision down the centre of his skull, like some Edwardian masher in the Hotel Bellevue all those years and years ago. '*Buon' diverti-mento*,' he said, which amused her. What sort of '*divertimento*' am I likely to find at my age? she felt like asking.

She inquired at the first kiosk, to which they usually went, but the woman shrugged her shoulders from inside her little box and then said that either the Sundays had not come or else, with all these foreign tourists, they must have sold out. She seemed neither to know nor care. Mrs Newman said '*Grazie*,' with a slight inclination of her head; but the woman had returned to her reading of *Oggi* and paid no attention.

The street up to the cathedral seemed far longer than she remembered it and there were so many people walking along, often arms linked or pushing prams or leading the large dogs that had recently become so fashionable. It was hard to avoid them and they often made no effort to avoid her. The handkerchief slipped off her forearm. After she had picked it up, stooping with difficulty on the crowded piazza, she decided not to replace it, since it must have gathered dust. She stuffed it into her bag. The dried blood had made it as crisp as a dead leaf.

She at last reached the kiosk by the cathedral. The Germans had got there before her and she waited patiently while they flicked over a magazine full of photographs of nude women and giggled and commented noisily. One of the boys would snatch the magazine from whoever was holding it and then it would be snatched in turn from him. They jostled and pushed each other while the girls looked on with indulgent smiles. At last Mrs Newman was able to get at the Sundays and paid out what seemed to be an exorbitant price for them. Almost two pounds, she reckoned. Then she began to hobble back. Yes, definitely, quite definitely, her ankle was swelling. But she had the Sundays, that gave her a quiet feeling of triumph.

She sat on a stone bench on the quay, a thin, bent, not particularly attractive old woman in a pink shantung dress, a pink straw hat and old-fashioned strap shoes, waiting for the hydrofoil to come skimming, an ungainly metallic swan, over the glittering water towards her. She did not look at the papers, which were far heavier than she had imagined to be possible. Instead, she stared at the lake, which seemed to widen as the sun mounted higher and higher above it, the mountains receding further and further into the pale blue sky, the villas and churches and little clusters of red-roofed houses receding further and further into the dark green foliage. She remembered a little *vaporetto* and a party of six of them, all young and all English; and how they had laughed at her because she had complained of feeling seasick on the short journey from the Hotel Bellevue to Como. A child with a hoop stopped and stared at her with a kind of brutal curiosity; and she stared back and then gave a tentative smile, which the child did not return. The child's mother screeched, laden with parcels: '*Mario! Vieni qua!*' and, with dragging footsteps and many backward glances, the child moved away, the hoop in one hand and the stick in the other.

Again the boatman helped her aboard. He said something about her returning very quickly and she felt too tired now to explain about the Sundays. So she just gave him a smile. After the confusion and noise of the journey out, the boat was now empty except for a couple, as old or older than herself, who sat very stiff, their arms close to their sides, without ever looking at each other or speaking to each other. Both wore black; the woman even had on black stockings and the man a black tie. Perhaps they were returning from or going to a funeral.

The *muletiere* seemed so steep, each cobble glistening, as though it were wet, in the sun that now shone full over the water, that she decided, having taken one or two steps, to turn back and take the road instead, even though it was longer. But she had forgotten that the road had no pavement; so that each time that a car whooshed past, she found herself cowering against the wall. It was silly of her, she knew that; there was plenty of room for the two of them. But she could not help herself, the reflex was too strong.

Suddenly she thought, Why shouldn't I try to hitchhike? From time to time her grandson did so, when he was too lazy to climb up from the beach or the shops to the villa. She halted and, when a little red beetle of a car, a Fiat 126, chugged round the bend below her, she made a vague poking gesture up the hill with her forefinger. The car screeched on. But the van that followed stopped. It belonged to the butcher, who, according to Mrs Newman's daughter, always put up his prices for them because they were foreigners. He was a stout, jolly man. She noticed that there were reddish stains round and under his fingernails, of blood she supposed, and that he smelled of raw meat. He asked where she had been and, when she told him, he said, '*E bello il giro*' and she said, Yes, yes indeed. She still felt too tired to try to tell him about the Sundays in her halting Italian.

'Where *have* you been, mother? You got us worried. I do wish you wouldn't just wander off like that.' Her daughter still lay out on the deckchair, her arms and legs and bare midriff glistening with oil.

'To Como.'

'To Como!' Her son-in-law also lay, almost naked, out in a deckchair. From inside she could hear that her grandson was playing one of his records. 'For God's sake, turn that down, can't you?' his father bawled.

'I got the Sundays for you.'

'Don't shout at him like that! These *are* his holidays, you know.'

'If he'd play something half-way decent! The Beatles would just be tolerable. But that crap hour by hour!'

There was the screech of the needle being jerked across the record; it sounded to Mrs Newman like someone tearing silk. The boy's face appeared, congested with rage, at the window. 'Can't I ever do anything I want to do?'

'Not if it conflicts with your dear father's wishes.'

'It's time you grew out of the Bay City Rollers. That's for kids.'

'I suppose you want me to listen to Beethoven symphonies all day. Not, I notice, that you've ever bought any.'

'Well, it would be an improvement.'

'Oh, do leave the poor boy alone!'

'I got the Sundays for you.'

No one seemed to hear her. The boy's angry face disappeared from the window. Her daughter replaced her mask over her eyes with a hand glistening with oil. Her son-in-law chewed on his pipe and squinted down at his detective story. She put the Sundays down on an empty deckchair and went into the house. She knew that none of them would pick them up; none of them would even glance at them. But, strangely, instead of feeling disappointment, she felt an exhilaration. I got them. It wasn't so difficult. In fact, it was rather fun. Quite a little adventure. The nicest day since, oh, I don't know when at this villa.

She put the stick back in its stand, glanced briefly at the graze on her forearm and then hobbled down the hall to the kitchen. As she expected, her daughter had put out the potatoes for her to peel. She always hated to have to do the potatoes herself and she had established this pretence that her mother enjoyed doing them. Mrs Newman began to peel, oblivious of the throbbing of her ankle; eventually the doctor would be summoned and would have to bind it up for her. As she peeled, she sang in a slightly cracked but still firm and true voice: 'Vilia, oh Vilia . . .' Yes, it had been a lovely morning. She couldn't remember such a lovely morning for a long, long time.

Out in the garden her daughter, son-in-law and grandson –

the boy had given up the record-player – listened for a few seconds. Then her son-in-law said: 'Mother seems to be in a very jaunty mood all of a sudden,' and her daughter said: 'I wonder what she's got to be so happy about.'

The Glass House

THROUGH the spy-hole, the profile of the girl appeared as in some hand-tinted Victorian photograph, the straight nose, the wide curve of the lips and the arc of an eyeb row all uncannily distinct but the thick, blond hair and the cartwheel of the straw hat blurred against the unfocused dazzle of sunlight on lilac leaves still glossy from the recent shower. Ruth could not see Tom, who must be standing two or three steps below the girl. Hand to latch, she thought: beautiful. For some reason she had not expected that beauty. Opulent and serene, it disconcerted her.

When she pulled back the door, so that the outside heat and brilliance fell, a clanging sheet of brass, into the murk of the hall, she all but cried out at the sudden transformation. The girl had turned her head from left to right and there, partly screened by the enormous hat, was this sickening sight of brownish, puckered skin, shrivelled mouth, eroded nostril, lashless eye, and an eyebrow that had been drawn in, with a pencil, in a single line that first curved upwards and then flew away grotesquely, almost to the temple.

'We've arrived.' The yellow tee-shirt had darkened to orange under Tom's armpits as he stood, feet turned outwards in that seemingly uncomfortable penguin stance of his, below the girl. A hand – Ruth had always found his stubby, muscular hands attractive, in spite of their bitten nails – rested on one of the girl's fragile arms, the ball of the thumb gently massaging the soft, blue-veined skin inside the crook, so that it wrinkled gently upwards.

'Tom! Lovely.' Ruth held out both her hands, the many rings on them, on ring finger, middle finger, even forefinger, glinting in the sunlight that was making her screw up her eyes. 'Oh, how lovely! It's been such an age.'

'This is Delia.'

'Delia. I've been wanting to meet you for a long, long time.'

'But I've known Tom for only six, oh seven, weeks!'

'Only! But I usually meet his girl-friends much sooner than that.'

Ruth's hand, hot and weighted with all that gold and all those gems, rested in the cool, light hand of the girl. Now she could see both halves of that face, the beauty and the horror. (Why did he never tell me? Usually he tells me *everything*.)

'Come in. Do.'

'What an enormous house! For London, I mean.' Removing the hat, with its length of grass-green chiffon tied around it, shaking out that thick, blond hair, hitching at a shoulder strap with an ungainly twist and raising of one shoulder. Tom took the hat from her and placed it on a chair (designed by William Morris, still the original fabric, the dark blue of the morning glories as worn and washed-out as his jeans). 'So cool,' the girl went on, in a low, breathy voice. 'Marvellous.'

'Yes, it *is* cool. I follow the Mediterranean practice. Draw all the blinds and shut all the windows from the first heat of day until the first cool of evening. It works – downstairs, at any rate. Come.' Ruth strutted down the passage and the boy and girl followed. The black lozenges of the tiles gleamed and the furniture, until ten days ago tirelessly polished by Ruth's ancient Spanish 'treasure' (sick now, perhaps dying, in St Mary Abbott's), gleamed also. The absurdly high heels under the plump, ageing woman, with her thin, reddish hair sticking up in front in a crest, went click, click, click, like the magnified sound of the claws of some bird.

'I love this room,' Tom said, not to Ruth, but to the girl. 'Each time that I come into it, I seem to come into it for the first time. There's so much to look at – furniture, pictures, knick-knacks, books – and nothing ever seems the same from one viewing to another. It's a pity you can't see the garden from the window at the moment.'

'Well, you can. If you want to.' Ruth smiled indulgently with what her children would call her 'nanny smile' and pulled at the cord of the venetian blind until there, beyond the glass, was the garden in which, so often while he was living with her, Tom would work at her side, the sweat trickling down the bony ridge of his spine and down the bony valley between the pink, prominent little nipples, each set in its cushion of white, gleaming musculature. Intentionally, she had allowed the garden to become overgrown, so that the prying neighbour on the other side of the low wall, an ancient woman, once a musical-comedy actress, in her neat beige slacks, her beige cashmere cardigan, and her pink wig, could no longer peer over it because of the tangle of ramblers and climbers, with a weeping willow drooping low above.

'Isn't it a lovely room?' Tom said to the girl.

Delia looked around her, shifting abruptly from one angle to another, through a whole jerky circle, as though not sure. A forefinger touched the corner of her mouth where, on the disfigured side, it puckered into no more than a thin line the colour of ash. 'Yes,' she said at last, with no certainty.

'Do sit.' Ruth extended her hands as though displaying the rings on them. 'Anywhere.'

'Don't you have a favourite chair?'

Ruth laughed. 'Do I look the sort of person who would have a favourite chair?' She was at the drinks cabinet. It had originally been an eighteenth-century Korean chest and, as she swung open one of its doors, heavy with its bosses of brass, she felt, as she always did, a pang of unease. Herman had had a cabinet maker transform it from its original use to its present one. Everyone had always remarked on Herman's taste and yet, from time to time, he was capable of something as tasteless as this.

The girl again jerked round in that circle and then moved over to the Victorian chaise-longue, its back a mahogany serpent of twining ivy and convolvulus, and lowered herself into it. She seemed to ponder a moment, before she unselfconsciously put up first one leg and then the other, crossing her small feet, in their flat-heeled slippers, at the ankle. Ruth felt a momentary annoyance, both because she feared that the slippers might soil the damask and because, though she had denied having a favourite seat, that chaise-longue was in fact her favourite – as Tom, of course, knew.

'What would you like to drink?'

'Well, what have you got?'

'Arsenic, cyanide, prussic acid.' But Ruth did not say that. Instead, she held up now this bottle and now this, listing them. At the end, Delia drawled in that low, breathy voice of hers, 'Well, what I think I'd *really* like is just a bitter lemon with lots and lots of ice.'

Tom carried over the drink. Delia sipped.

'To your taste? Enough ice?'

'Super.'

'The usual for you?' Ruth said to Tom, her small hands scrabbling in the ice bucket. She began to pour out the Pimm's No. 1, before he replied. She knew that she did not have to wait for a reply since all through the summer that he had lodged in the house he had never asked for anything else. 'I haven't any of the fruit cut up for you, I'm afraid. Remiss of me. Just the mint and the lemon.'

'Oh, that's fine. I don't need the usual fruit salad. We must have a good appetite for dinner.'

Ruth poured out some sherry for herself and went and sat in a straight-backed chair, with her back to the window, her legs crossed high.

'I thought we might go to that Indian restaurant,' she said. 'In hot weather, I love a curry.'

In fact, she hated a curry, in hot weather most of all. But when Tom had telephoned from Brighton to say that he had been paid a bonus and wanted to take her out, she had thought, Well, any bonus paid to him can't be much, and had then decided that the best course would be to steer him in the direction of the Indian

C

restaurant round the corner, its purple flock paper encrusted with dust, its tablecloths stained orange from the messes of previous diners, and its lavatories stinking of ammonia at the end of a low-ceilinged corridor scrawled with graffiti.

'Oh, Christ, I'm not going to take you to that dump. No, I've booked somewhere quite different.'

'Somewhere quite different? Where?'

'Wait and see. It's to be a surprise. I bet you've been there before. But still.' He turned to Delia: 'She's been everywhere.'

'A surprise! How lovely. But I hope it's nowhere terribly expensive.'

'I want to give you a really good dinner. In celebration.'

Ruth thought: In celebration? Of what? Of meeting this girl? Of shacking up with her? Of deciding to marry her?

'Ruth was so good to me when I was going through my difficult time.' He was now perching on the edge of the chaise-longue, lifting the girl's feet, still crossed at the ankles, on to his lap. 'It *was* a difficult time. Wasn't it, Ruth?'

Ruth thought of those days when he would lie, silent and motionless, on his bed high up on the attic floor of the house, refusing to answer her when she would say, 'What's the matter? Are you ill? Are you unhappy? What is it?' and pushing aside any food that she carried to him. She thought of the jobs that he took and then, inexplicably, after two or three days, would return from, often in late morning or mid-afternoon, as though the owner of the restaurant, sandwich-bar or boutique could no longer stand his presence or he could no longer stand the proximity of anyone but her. She thought of the often unpaid rent ('Oh, don't worry about it, forget it!') and of the mess that he would leave in the kitchen, bathroom and even in this sitting-room, where he would sprawl on that chaise-longue, his pale grey eyes expressionless as he stared at the television for numbing hour after hour.

'Yes, I suppose it was a difficult time. Yes.'

'You were so good to me.' Turning to Delia: 'She was so good to me. You wouldn't credit. No landlady can ever have been so good to any lodger.'

'I never thought of you as a lodger.'

Many of her closest friends had assumed him to be her lover. Why else did she put up with him? She must be lonely, they would tell each other – even with her painting. Husband dead, both children abroad, isolated in that large, eccentric house on the breast of the hill, with its trees so dense around it.

'I want to make you some kind of return. Not a really adequate return for all you did for me, but as adequate as I can make it.'

The girl sipped delicately at her drink and then looked up from it. 'People are never kind just for the sake of being kind. Are they?' She looked first at Tom, then at Ruth.

Ruth thought: The bitch! What was she getting at? Probably what Marietta – Ruth's sister, now married, for the third time, to a rancher in Texas – had so often been getting at. There was that afternoon, yes, when Tom had come into the murk of this same room from the dazzle of the garden and had announced sulkily, 'I can't do any more of that weeding. It's far too hot.' Ruth had smiled indulgently, as he had stood before them, stripped to the waist, and had said, 'Well, of course, my dear, you needn't do any more. Do just as much as you want – or as little.' He had gone out at that. And then, her hands clasped together between her knees, Marietta had leant forward, saliva glistening on her pendulous lower lip. 'Oh,' she had exclaimed. 'Oh, oh. What H. on E.!'

It was years since either of the sisters had used that phrase to the other. H. on E. – heaven on earth. So Marietta, too, had felt his attraction and had known that Ruth must feel it.

'He's so skinny,' Ruth had said, angrily dismissive.

But Marietta had laughed, throwing back her head, while she still clasped her hands between her knees, like some little girl afraid of wetting herself. 'Oh, come. Come. I envy you.'

Now the girl was asking: 'Do you live all by yourself in this huge house?'

'Yes.' Ruth nodded. 'Except for my Spanish treasure. And she's ill at the moment. In hospital. I sometimes feel rather ashamed about it,' she went on, wondering why she should feel any need to excuse herself to this stranger. 'After Tom, I had another lodger. But, well, it was not the same thing. We never got on to the same wavelength somehow.'

'And you and Tom did. Well, I can see that you did!' The girl laughed. 'How many rooms do you have here?'

'Oh, I don't know. I've no idea. I've never counted.' Silly answer. Of course she knew. But she was determined not to give way to this prying, any more than to the prying of that pink-wigged neighbour on the other side of the low wall.

'It's beautifully cool in here.'

'Yes, it is, isn't it? The downstairs of this house is always cool. But upstairs – in a heatwave like this one, it becomes sheer hell. And in the winter . . . you've no idea what the radiators cost.'

Tom began gently to stroke one of the girl's shins, as, on the doorstep, he had stroked the inside of the crook of her arm, the ball of his thumb travelling gently up and down. 'You should have got rid of those night-storage heaters long ago. They're hopelessly extravagant.'

'Yes, I know, I know. Another of Herman's mistakes.' She turned to Delia. 'Herman was my husband.'

'A famous architect,' Tom put in.

'For a famous architect, he made an awful lot of mistakes. This house is in so many of the books and yet it's the exact opposite of the machine for living that it's supposed to be.'

'It's beautiful,' the girl said. 'Beautiful, if strange.'

'Beautiful. Yes. But on days like these I simply can't use my studio.'

'Why not?'

'Why not?' (How obtuse she was being.) 'Well, because the studio runs the whole length of the floor below the attics and it's just too hot up there. Unbearable. I'd fry. All that glass, you see. At first this house used to be known as "The Grass House", because Grass was my husband's name. But now everyone calls it "The Glass House".' Ruth frowned. 'Hopeless for insulation.'

'And hopeless if you want to throw stones. Though I'm sure you never do.' The girl sipped again and, as she did so, Ruth was suddenly, inexplicably certain – just as, many years ago, in this same room, she was suddenly, inexplicably certain of Herman's infidelity – of the girl's hatred of her.

'I've often thought of selling the house,' Ruth said untruth-fully, having never thought of it, despite the urgings of her children, her friends and Marietta. 'But who would buy it? Some Arab, perhaps.'

'Was your husband a refugee?'

'Yes.'

'From Germany?'

'No. The Netherlands.'

'Jewish?'

'Yes. Why?'

'I thought he must have been.'

'How did you and Tom meet each other?' Ruth already knew, because Tom had written to tell her how he had met this girl serving in the wine bar opposite the antique shop at which he worked; but vindictively she now wanted to make the little slut herself come out with the story.

'Tom must have told you. Didn't you, Tom?'

'I – I think so.'

'Well.' Delia smiled and sipped again. Then she said: 'You paint.' It was not a question.

'Yes, I paint. It helps to pass the time. There seems a lot of it to pass.' Ruth despised herself for not having the pride to answer, 'Yes, I paint, and I paint bloody well, and though you may not have heard of me, others, more cultivated, have.'

The girl turned her head sideways to gaze out of the window, so that Ruth was once again forced either to avert her eyes or to re-examine that brownish, puckered flesh, with the horrible shrivelling of lips, nostril and eyelid. 'I saw something of yours. Once. Somewhere. I rather liked it.'

'Thank you.' Ruth turned to Tom: 'Did you book a table?'

'Of course.' He laughed. 'This is the sort of restaurant where you *have* to book a table, I imagine.'

'I do hope it's not going to be terribly expensive.'

'Why worry?' Now Delia was showing her other profile, the one that made her look like a Du Maurier girl in a Punch cartoon. 'He's going to pay.'

'I know that.' Ruth was tart. 'But I don't want him to pay too much. I hate to see money thrown away on food.'

'Is that any worse than throwing it away on anything else? On heating, for instance?' The girl swung her legs down off Tom's lap. 'I'd like to see the portrait,' she announced.

'What portrait?'

'The one of Tom. He said you did one of him once.'

'Well, I started one. But I never completed it. He left for Brighton before I had time. I'm such a slow worker.'

Hour after hour he had sat motionless beside that window for her. They had rarely spoken. ('Tired?' 'No. Are you?' 'No, not really.' 'A drink?' 'Not yet.' 'What's that colour you're using?' 'Burnt sienna.' 'Oh.') But as she had recharged her brush, gazed at him, gazed at the canvas, dabbed here or made a stroke there, she had had an extraordinary sense of communion and propinquity. They had never been so close; probably they would never again be so close.

'May I see it?'

'Oh, I don't think – '

'Show it to her,' Tom urged, 'do show it to her.'

'Oh. All right.'

Ruth got up, feeling suddenly weary and ill-tempered and wishing that the evening were over. 'It's upstairs,' she said. She sighed: 'So far.'

Tom jumped up. 'I'll get it.'

'You won't know where to find it.'

'Of course I will.'

'It's stacked beneath the window.'

'I know, I know!'

He had gone and the girl was leaning forward on the chaise-longue, her thin hands clasped together round one of her knees. 'He's still devoted to you.'

'How nice.' Ruth was dry. 'And I'm still devoted to him.'

'He often talks about you.'

'I often think about him. Is he happier now?'

The girl nodded, as if to say: 'With *me*? Of course he is!'

Ruth got up and wandered out into the hall. She could not bear this closeness to so much pent-up hostility without Tom there as some kind of shield. But the girl followed her, her slippers making a soft, slurping sound on the black, highly polished tiles.

'Have you found it?' Ruth shouted up.

'Yep.' Tom came racing down the stairs, so violently that Ruth could feel the banister shaking under her hand as it rested there. Suddenly, everything seemed to be shaking, as though in an earthquake. It was as though the high, handsome house were about to tumble down around them.

'Here.' He held out the portrait.

Ruth took it from him and placed it on the William Morris chair. Head tilted to one side, she said: 'I think that's the best place to view it. You get the light from above.'

The girl studied the portrait of the young man, now her young man and once Ruth's young man, as he sat, stripped to the waist, and looked out at them with a desolately vacant gaze from a frame of stiff, glossy leaves, crowding all around him. 'I've seen him like that,' she said at last. 'But not often.'

'It's not finished,' Ruth said.

'But you'll finish it one day.'

Ruth shrugged, putting a hand to the edge of the canvas and tilting it away from her. 'That depends on Tom. I've always wanted to finish it.'

Tom said: 'I like it as it is.'

Delia turned away, as though the portrait had now lost all interest for her. 'You don't often paint people, do you?'

'No. Not often.'

Ruth returned to the room, leaving the portrait still on the chair, and the others followed her, their hands linked.

'Did your husband know Tom?' Ruth was now refilling Delia's glass, with the girl uncomfortably, even menacingly, close beside her.

'No. Oh, dear no. He was dead long before Tom came into my life.'

'Thanks.' The girl took the glass held out to her. 'I wonder what he would have made of him,' she said.

'I think he would have liked him. He liked most people.'

The girl sipped. 'And there's so much to like in Tom.'

'Yes. So much.'

The girl now began to wander about the room, examining the things crowded into it – some enormously valuable, some of no value at all – with the air of a viewer at an auction sale. Tom smiled at Ruth, raising an eyebrow, as though to ask, 'Well, what do you think of her?' Ruth turned away.

'Who helps you with the garden now? In my place, I mean.'

'No one. I do it all alone.'

'So I wasn't indispensable!'

He was being as cruel as the girl; but Ruth knew that, unlike her, he had no intention of being cruel.

Suddenly the girl broke off her examination of the contents of the room and said, not to Ruth, but to Tom: 'Where's the loo? I must spend a penny.'

'I'll show you.'

He went out with her, then returned, shutting the door carefully behind him.

'Well?' It was as much a challenge as a question.

'She's . . .' Ruth hesitated. Then: 'I like her.' (What else could she say?)

'It's made such a difference to my life, meeting her like that. Before – I wondered if I could stick it out in the shop, stick it out in Brighton. Part of me kept hankering to be back here with you.'

Ruth could not restrain herself from asking the question: 'Her face?'

'Awful.' He turned away, to gaze at the same stiff, glossy leaves that crowded round him in the portrait. 'An accident. When she was a baby. She fell into a fire.'

'*Fell?*'

'Or was pushed. No one really knows. She won't talk about it. I once tried to get her to. But . . .' He shrugged.

'How ghastly!'

He nodded. 'But she's so beautiful in spite of it. Or because of it, I sometimes think.' He looked at her dubiously: 'Isn't she?'

Ruth nodded. 'Yes. She's beautiful.'

'The moment I saw her . . .'

They heard Delia out in the hall and, as though guilty of their proximity before the window, simultaneously moved apart. But the girl did not enter. (Perhaps, her ear to the door, she's trying to learn what we have to say to each other or even – yes, why not? – what we have meant or still mean to each other.) Tom licked his lips, his tongue travelling over them as though, in growing alarm, he were tasting something bitter and caustic. (Is it poison, is it not poison?)

Ruth said boldly: 'Dear Tom.' (Let the bitch hear, if she wanted to hear!) 'Why have you left it so long to come and see me?'

'I *had* to. Don't you see?'

No, she didn't see; or she didn't want to admit that she saw.

The girl entered demurely, eyes lowered. 'I love your loo,' she said. She was smelling of the Chanel that Ruth, hurrying to get ready for them after a bath, had left out on her dressing-table in her bedroom. (So she's been spying out the territory!)

'Yes. My husband bought that marvellous Victorian lavatory basin and the mahogany surround from a builder for a fiver. It came from a house that was being modernized just below this one. It works far better than any modern loo – but it uses three times as much water.'

'I see what you mean about the heat upstairs.

'As I said, it's all that glass.'

The girl turned to Tom: 'Shouldn't we be setting out? We don't want to miss our table.'

'I do wish you'd settled for the Indian restaurant. I love it. I don't want anywhere too grand.'

'Only the best for you,' Tom said.

'Yes, only the best for you,' the girl echoed with malicious sarcasm.

When Tom paid off their taxi, he managed to scatter the coins – fivepence pieces, twopenny pieces, penny pieces, halfpenny pieces – that he had drawn out of the pockets of his jeans, in a shower across the pavement and even into the gutter. The girl watched, smirking slightly, while he and Ruth stooped to pick them up. Then she said: 'They're worth *nothing* nowadays. Why bother?'

Ruth straightened. 'But you can't take us here. It's one of the most expensive restaurants in London.'

'That's precisely why I chose it.'

Tom was holding the coins in the palm of his hand and, as Ruth added those that she herself had retrieved, she wanted to demand of him: 'And how do you expect to settle the bill? Those bits of metal that you're clutching there won't be much use to you.' Dear Tom! It was heartbreaking, as well as idiotic. Like that time when he had just drawn his dole money and went out and bought her a bottle of Birnenwasser, because she had happened to say that she so much preferred it to brandy. She made a final effort: 'Oh, do let's go somewhere else! There's a pizza place just around the corner.' (Revolting. Her son, always mean, had taken her there on one of his leaves from Kenya.)

'I've absolutely no intention of taking you to a pizza place. Don't be silly, Ruth!'

'Yes, sir?' Though he was probably some Italian, Greek or Spanish peasant, the waiter, with his sleek hair and sinuous movements, put all the supercilious irony of which he was capable into the two words. It was a long time since Ruth had been the guest of a man who was welcomed in that fashion. It took her back to the year before the war, when Herman, then an impoverished and shabby refugee, would take her (she having previously given him the money) to the Café Royal or the Criterion Grill.

Tom blushed, stammered. 'I . . . I booked a table.'

'Yes, sir?' The interrogative was again subtly insulting. 'What name, sir?'

It was then that the astonishing thing happened. From the far end of the restaurant, its *sang de bœuf* walls crowded with sporting prints in vulgarly shiny gilt frames, the manager – yes, it must be the manager in that blue blazer with its gold buttons and those cream trousers widely flared at the bottoms – raised both pudgy hands and hurried over. Ruth thought that it was she whom he had recognized, though she could not imagine why; but it was to the girl that he now cried out near-falsetto, in an Italian accent: 'Signorina Delia! Long time, no see!'

'Hello, Lauro.' She was coolly patronizing.

'This way. You will be nice an' fresh over 'ere. By the garden. Please!'

As he pulled back one of the spindly gilt chairs, not for Ruth but for Delia, he turned to summon a plumper, greyer man, in similar blazer and trousers: 'Hey! Giovanni! Look 'oo's 'ere. Signorina Delia!'

'Signorina Delia!' The other man now bustled over. 'Your daddy – Sir 'enry – was 'ere for lunch only yesterday. Long time, no see!' He put out a hand and the girl took it with the same cool condescension that she had shown to his partner.

'Where you been all this time?' the younger Italian asked.

'In Brighton. I've got a job there.'

'Brighton! Lovely!' He snatched a napkin, shook it out with a flourish and then handed it to her. 'I 'ave your favourite dish. Salmon trout.'

'Oh, Lauro, how super!'

When both Italians finally had left them, Ruth said: 'So they know you here.'

'Oh, yes. I often come here with my father. He works just round the corner – or, rather, round two corners.'

Ruth wanted to ask: 'Who is your father? What does he do?'
But she restrained herself.

Tom leant across the table, smiling proudly. 'Delia's well
known to them all. Actually it was her suggestion that I should
bring you here.'

'I see.'

'As you know, I don't know much about restaurants. Not this
kind, anyway. Just not my scene.'

The wine waiter now appeared and held out the list to Ruth.
'Madame would like to order some wine?'

Ruth passed the list on to Tom. 'The host had better
choose.'

'Oh, Christ! Delia – *you* choose!'

'All right.' Coolly she took the list and glanced down it.
'Since I'm having the salmon trout and you're both having
chicken, how about a Chablis?'

'Sounds fine. Ruth?'

'Yes, that sounds perfect.'

Delia smiled up at the wine waiter. 'Number 12,' she said.
'But it must be really chilled.'

'Of course, madame. Well chilled. Of course.'

As though the victory of this surprising welcome had appeased
the demon previously raging within her, the girl suddenly
became the most attentive and charming of companions. 'I
wonder what your husband would have made of this décor. A
marvellous example of ghastly good taste. But the food is first
rate.'

'Yes. I've eaten here before. But a long time ago. I so seldom
eat out now.'

Over her avocado vinaigrette: 'I do hope you'll finish his
portrait.'

Over her salmon trout, delicately removing a bone between
thumb and forefinger: 'I love your house. It's a dream house,
whatever you may say about it.'

Over her *mousse au chocolat*: 'This is fun!'

Tom smiled, smiled, smiled. It was all working out all right after all. It was all as he had hoped it would be, and not as he had feared it would be.

Ruth thought: Well, it was natural that, at first, there should have been all that barely suppressed hostility. Why not? No doubt the girl had convinced herself, as so many others had done, that during the previous summer, even hotter than this one, Tom had been her prisoner, not her patient, in the Glass House.

When the waiter brought the bill, he set it down before Ruth. 'No, no!' Tom cried out, snatching at the plate, while Ruth countered, 'But, Tom, why not let me do it? Please!'

Tom looked down at the bill, gaped and paled.

'I'm sure it's huge. At least let me give you half.'

'Of course not.' From the back pocket of his jeans he pulled out a credit-card. He had certainly not possessed one during the months that he had lived with her. 'This will deal with it – for five or six weeks, at any rate.'

'I do wish – '

'No!'

Out in the street, he asked: 'Shall I get you a taxi? We can't see you home, because we must catch our train to Brighton. I'm sorry.'

'Tom, I think we'll have to take a taxi ourselves,' Delia put in, linking her arm in his. 'Otherwise that train will go without us.'

As Tom flagged down a taxi, staggering out into the road, Ruth suddenly realized that, having consumed most of the Chablis and then having had a brandy, he must now be drunk. He had always had the weakest of heads.

'Come!' he called over his shoulder to Ruth.

'No, you both take it. I think I'd like some fresh air. I'll walk a little.'

'Really?'

'Yes, really. Hurry!'

He lurched back to her, leaving Delia by the taxi. 'Goodbye, Ruth. I do hope you enjoyed the evening – well, at least half as much as I did.'

'Every bit as much.'

He put an arm round her shoulder, so that she could smell the sweat of the day heavy on him; then he put his lips to her cheek.

'Dear Tom!'

The girl waved from the taxi, one foot raised as she was about to step in. Then, as Tom hurried over to her, she lowered the foot and herself returned to Ruth. 'I'm so glad to have met you. I thought – to be frank – that we might not hit it off, but it's been super, absolutely super. I've loved every moment of it.' (Ruth thought: Is she also drunk?) Suddenly, she threw both arms around the older woman, pressing one side of her face, the hideously disfigured side, against one side of Ruth's. Involuntarily, Ruth drew in her breath and, as she did so, again smelled that Chanel. Then, with an effort, she forced herself to kiss the bronze, puckered flesh. 'Let's meet again,' she said.

'Oh, yes, yes!'

The girl began to hurry back to the taxi, where Tom stood waiting for her. She waved: 'Now take care! Don't come to any harm!'

'Oh, I'm not nervous of muggers. I walk everywhere at night.'

But the two of them had already disappeared inside the taxi.

The room high up in the Glass House seemed intolerably hot after the coolness of the night-time streets. Dear Tom, she thought. Dear, dear Tom. It was a kind of end, of course. A celebration, as he had called it, but also a wake. Probably she would never see him again without that girl; and probably, even with her she would now see him less and less. It was even possible – she faced the fact with the calm stoicism with which Herman had faced his imminent death – that she would never see him again. But, in his own way, Tom had carried it all off with the same style that Herman had brought to the process of leaving her, the Glass House and the world. Style. That was what she always admired and loved in others. She had not thought Tom capable of it.

She lay out uncovered on the bed, as the heat swirled in

giddying waves around her. It must be one of the hottest August nights for years. Eventually she slept; then half-slept; then lay awake again, the sweat pouring off her. Yes, they were right, her children and her friends, she must leave the Glass House and move to somewhere smaller and more practical. A machine for living, a machine for dying. One froze in winter, one fried in summer. She dropped off again and then woke, her heart hammering with an inexplicable terror, to find that the sheet, previously thrown back, was now wound stickily round and round her, like some monstrous bandage. She put a hand out for the tumbler of water that she always kept on her bedside table and gulped from it. Lukewarm, brackish, as though from some stagnant pond. Disgusting. She could feel the sweat crawl between her breasts and the memory came back to her of the garden, dark green under a molten sky, and the sweat trickling down the bony ridge of Tom's spine and then down the bony valley of his chest, as he toiled away beside her. H. on E. Heaven on earth, hell on earth.

At a few minutes past five, she dragged herself from the bed and decided to go down the beautiful circular staircase, the core of the house, to the room that gave out on to the garden. It must surely be cooler there. But with each step that she descended, the giddying, sickening heat intensified, as though she were making her way down and down towards the heart of a volcano. Silly house, silly Herman. How *could* it be so hot at this hour?

It was as she passed down the hall, her nightdress floating around her, that a blast on her bare leg made her realize that the night-storage heater was on; and not merely on but turned up full to 5, where she never had it even in the depth of winter. She stooped to the switch and clicked it off and only then thought with despair: Much good will that do, it'll hold the heat all day. Bewildered, she remained beside the radiator, seeking for an explanation.

Eventually, she laboured back up the stairs and, on the landing above, stooped and laid a hand on the heater there. It, too, was burning; she pulled away her hand and gently rubbed the scorched palm. In the bathroom, the same. On the landing above, the same. In her bedroom, the same.

Suddenly, she recalled how long Delia had been absent when she had gone up to the lavatory; and then there came back to her that odour of Chanel both when she had eventually returned to join them and when, later in the evening, she had pressed the disfigured side of her face against Ruth's.

It was horrifying, the malice of it, and yet, in a curious way, satisfying, since she was now free to hate the girl, as she had all along wanted to do and had yet been guilty of wanting. Fry, fry, fry. Fry in this hell that your architect husband built for you, just as so many of his family fried in the gas ovens. That had been her intention.

Ruth went downstairs again, circling into the heart of the volcano that the girl had created for her, and then walked on into the sitting-room, where she threw open the french windows into the garden. She went out, feeling, with a wonderful relief, the dawn air cold on her burning forehead, her sticky nightdress, between her breasts, and on her bare arms. Wonderful. She would have to spend the whole day out here, under the shade of the trees, until the bricks in each of those bloody heaters had cooled. She lay out on a hammock and, as she lay there, her hands clasped in her lap, the fever of her panic and rage was succeeded by a chill of despair. Tom was lost to her. Oh yes. Irrevocably. In the early light, the leaves crowding all around her seemed all at once to have acquired the weight and sheen of metal. They threatened to crush her. If she put out a hand and pushed at one of the branches, it would surely clang against the branch nearest to it.

Later, much later, as the birds began to trill and shrill more and more loudly and the huge tawny tom cat belonging to the woman with the pink wig crept stealthily over the wall, its topaz eyes glinting with the pleasure of the chase, she went back into the house to get herself a glass of milk. It was as she returned with it, from the kitchen to the hall, that the realization came to her: Something is missing. Something. What?

She gazed all around her. All her possessions, the things of enormous value and the things of no value at all, seemed to be in place. But something, something. Think. *Think*.

She stared at the washed-out morning glories on the William Morris chair, feeling, against her shins and thighs, the heat from the night-storage heater blowing out in wave on giddying wave. Then she remembered. *Of course!* The portrait, *his* portrait. Could the girl have stolen it? It had been on the chair and now it was no longer on the chair. Could she? But how, how?

She searched back and forth, upstairs and downstairs and even in the cellars, while that heat once more made her feel giddy and sick and once more caused the sweat to pour off her body.

Then she glimpsed it. Behind the night-storage heater in the hall. Pushed there.

Carefully, she eased it out. It was so hot that she could hardly bear to touch it. It was scorched, the paint blistered and puckered, the colours streaked with orange and brown. It was unrecognizable except that, having lain there tilted at an angle, it still preserved an eye, a cheek, a nostril and a faint curve of lips in all their former beauty.

Blindness

WHEN, at a dinner-party given by her parents soon after her return from Bolivia, Irene was asked what her life there had been like, she replied: 'Well, rather like living on the landing.' The guests had been puzzled, until she had explained: an *au pair* belonged neither upstairs nor downstairs but somewhere in between. Then everyone had laughed, since Irene so manifestly belonged, here in her parents' manor house, 'upstairs'.

A young man with a drooping moustache and drooping shoulders queried: 'Why did you ever accept the job?'

'Because I wanted to see what South America was like. And because I wanted to see what life on the landing – if not downstairs – was like too.'

'You must have had lots of adventures?' a woman friend of Irene's mother put in. Ravaged and rouged, she herself had had lots of adventures, upstairs, on the landing and even downstairs; but all that was now behind her – or beneath her – since she had married an impoverished Labour peer.

Irene thought about the question. 'Well, not really,' she answered. 'I was in a motor accident and I was thrown from a horse – but in neither case did I break any bones. I had no love affairs, if that's what you mean.' Everyone laughed, except her questioner, who had indeed meant precisely that. 'Oh, and yes, I saw a lot of Adriana Valera.'

The guests looked at each other, puzzled. Who was Adriana Valera? A famous actress, dancer, film star? Or the wife of one of those generals or admirals who were forever seizing power in countries like Bolivia? Only one of the guests remembered that she was a famous poet, perhaps the most famous that her country had ever produced, and that many years before, when someone on the Nobel Prize Committee had asked, 'Have we ever given the prize to any Bolivian writer?', it was she who had received it. The man who remembered this was editor of a Sunday supplement; and he at once thought that possibly – since Adriana Valera must be centuries old by now, and extreme old age, like extreme youth, was a saleable commodity – Irene might be encouraged to write something about this friendship. In thinking that it was a friendship, he was in fact wrong; for though Irene had seen the old woman day after day for several months on end, it was dependence, not friendship, that had been so imperiously thrust on her.

Adriana Valera was now blind; and since all her life she had had a passion for English poetry – for Tennyson, Browning, Arnold and Swinburne above all – and since she could not bear to hear such authors read to her falteringly in the accents of her own country, she was always eager to enlist some English resident – a journalist or visiting writer, the wife of a businessman, an Embassy secretary or even a shorthand typist – to read to her instead. Because she was the aunt of the tin baron to whose children Irene had to speak English, it was inevitable that she should press the English girl into service too.

After the death, more than a half-century before, of a husband of whom no one seemed to know anything other than that he had been much older than his wife and had bequeathed to her vast, uncultivated tracts of the country, Adriana had lived, between her restless travels, always in the same mansion opposite one Embassy and next to another. Though she was tended by innumerable servants, the men in white jackets and gloves and the women in black dresses and white aprons, there was a frugality about the way in which she would offer Irene no more than a cup of tea, poured out of a silver teapot by a shrivelled, yellowing woman to whom she always referred as 'my nurse', and one or two moist, crumbling biscuits. There was never any question of payment for all the hours that Irene devoted to her; and when Irene said her last goodbye before returning home to

England, the only present that the poetess had given her was a handkerchief sachet, embroidered by 'my nurse'. Since Adriana had often told Irene irritably to blow her nose and not to sniff, Irene wondered whether there was malice, as well as meanness, in this choice of gift.

Yet, in retrospect, she knew that her happiest hours had been those spent in the vast, gloomy drawing-room of that mansion, her voice echoing in its high vaulted ceiling as she yet again read 'Tithonus' or 'Dover Beach' or 'My Last Duchess' or 'The Garden of Proserpine'. If the voice was not loud enough to produce that echo, then Adriana would chide her, her blind eyes, disconcerting because they seemed to be healthy, fixed on some spot just above and beyond her head: 'Don't mumble, my dear!' The near-nonagenarian was now also getting deaf.

It was not this reading that Irene enjoyed – she had always hated both reading to others and being read to – but, between one poem or story and another, the talk. Of this talk, Irene produced almost nothing; but that did not worry her, since she had never been a talkative person. It was as if the old woman, so heavily draped and shawled in even the hottest weather, was, despite all appearances, some supremely gifted child, playing with an inexhaustible lego kit of memories and ideas. 'Sit down, look at me, see what I can do,' that supremely gifted child seemed to be saying to the English visitor; and then, swift as thought, she would join one piece of lego to another and another to that.

Irene would often wonder: Does she know who I am? What I look like? My age? My interests? Adriana had never questioned Irene about any of these things and it was doubtful if she had ever questioned anyone else about them. If on some rare occasion, Irene ventured something about herself, Adriana would abruptly cut her off – usually with what Irene had come to call one of her 'lecturettes'; and since these 'lecturettes' were all so fascinating – erudite, lambent with a playful irony, barbed with a malicious wit – Irene never felt that she had any cause for complaint.

There were also the reminiscences: and these, even more than the lecturettes, held Irene spellbound. As a young woman, Adriana had had to repulse an advance from Rodin, had travelled with Henry James in Edith Wharton's 'fiery chariot', and had been brought an eighteen-page letter from Proust by Antoine Bibesco. As an old woman, she had had to give Ernest Hemingway 'a lesson in manners' when he had stayed with her, had walked the Backs with E. M. Forster and 'a far from beautiful or youthful companion', and had been given 'an outrageously amorous' tomcat by Colette.

The only parts of Adriana's endless, deep-voiced talk that bored Irene were her boastings of her achievements on behalf of exploited and enslaved womanhood both in Bolivia and in the other countries of South America. Perhaps Irene would have been spellbound by these too, if she had not heard the peremptory tone with which the old woman would command 'my nurse' and the other servants; had not observed their blatant terror of their mistress; and had not – on one occasion when a bell had not been answered and she had been dispatched to find out why – been obliged to venture into the murky, low-ceilinged warren at the back of the vestibule and there seen for herself how the staff existed, themselves exploited and, yes, enslaved.

When the editor of the Sunday supplement pressed her yet again for a piece – he had by now learned that Adriana was about to celebrate her ninetieth birthday – Irene eventually wrote down all this and much else for him. He then dispatched a photographer to La Paz, who returned with some excellent photographs of the blind old sybil, looking unexpectedly benign, as she sat stiffly in a straight-backed chair, rug over bony knees and shawl over bony shoulders – how well Irene remembered that pose, though not that expression of benignity – while 'my nurse' and the other servants hovered smiling in the background. The photographs all suggested a happy family – indeed, that was the expression used in one of the captions – instead of a group of prisoners and their gaoler. The article was also accompanied by a photograph of Irene herself, flanked by two of her parents' labradors, as, dressed in tweeds, ribbed woollen stockings and flat-heeled shoes, she stood, vaguely self-conscious, before the Gloucestershire manor house. The mention that she had been in La Paz as an *au pair* had been deleted from her article, so that any reader might have supposed merely that a moneyed, aristocratic and attractive girl had, for some eccentric reason, decided to make her abode there for a year.

Friends commended the piece. One aunt said dubiously: 'Now that you've started, dear, I suppose you'll go on.' An unknown American academic, on a sabbatical in England, rang up, having got hold of Irene's number from the Sunday supplement, and asked if he could come and talk about Adriana, since he was engaged on a book about her; but Irene replied that she really had nothing more to say than she had said already and that there would therefore be little point. A French literary journal published a translation, for which it never paid.

But there were also two objectors. A man, of whom Irene had never heard but who was evidently a fan and perhaps even a friend of Adriana, wrote in to the newspaper that published the Sunday supplement to say that, though it had clearly been hurtful for Irene not to have the poetess 'hang on to her lips', she ought to have realized, firstly, that she was now not merely blind but also extremely deaf, and, secondly, that most people would have felt privileged even to sit totally silent in such a presence. Clearly, whereas Adriana could not read because she was blind, this man did not read because he was lazy. Nowhere had Irene written that her enforced silence had been hurtful to her.

The other objection came obliquely in the course of a review of a book by a well-known woman novelist, a champion of Women's Lib, who had written about her travels in South America as a lecturer for the British Council. Apparently, while in La Paz, she had, on an impulse, telephoned to Adriana and had at once been invited round to the house. There had then sprung up 'a miraculous understanding' between the two of them, Except on those occasions when the English writer was lecturing, she had spent every waking hour in Adriana's company – walking with her through the parks of La Paz, talking with her in restaurants, and reading to her by her bedside. (Irene had never once heard of Adriana visiting a park or a restaurant and had never once herself been admitted to her bedroom.) 'I was sorely tempted to offer myself to her as her Boswell,' the writer recorded. 'But then I thought of my husband and my children and my books – poor things in comparison with hers but none the less mine own – and I reluctantly restrained myself.'

The reviewer of this volume of travel described the account of the relationship with Adriana as 'its highlight'. It was so humorous and yet so touching; there was such piquancy in the contrast between the beautiful young English novelist, still fighting the battles of her sex, and the distinguished nonagenarian, whose battles were behind her; each of the participants in this extraordinary friendship had clearly suffered a *coup de foudre* – except that, in these post-Freudian times, to say that could lead to all kinds of misunderstanding. The reviewer then went on: 'After a recent article in which the young author, also a woman, did everything in her power to diminish one of the great literary figures of our century, how pleasurable it is to read this so much more generous and kindly appraisal!'

Irene read the review over breakfast and she knew at once that that last paragraph could refer only to herself. How unfair! She had felt absolutely no desire to score off Adriana; to punish her for her total lack of interest in anything but herself, her own ideas and her own memories; to express any dissatisfaction that all those hours of reading had been rewarded – those cups of lukewarm tea, those crumbling biscuits and that handkerchief sachet apart – with nothing more tangible than a fascinating presence and fascinating talk. Oh, yes, how unfair!

She set off for a walk with the labradors, in order to clear her mind of the injustice; and it was only then, as the two dogs pursued something invisible in a tangle of spinney, that suddenly a memory awakened in her.

Adriana had been talking about Virginia Woolf, whom she had known, and about *A Room of One's Own*.

Irene then made one of her rare interjections: Had she also read *Not Just a Room of One's Own*?

Adriana had frowned in displeasure, as she did when anyone attempted to dam the flood of her talk, and had shaken her head.

Well, Irene had gone on, it was by this woman novelist, really very good, who – well, who wrote a lot about Women's Lib and things of that kind. (Irene always tended to be inarticulate on the few occasions when Adriana allowed her to say something.)

And what was this writer's name?

Irene had told her.

The old woman had then screwed up those blind eyes and pursed those still beautiful lips, in an effort at remembrance. 'I seem to remember the name,' she had said dubiously; and then she had gone on to talk about that wonderful occasion when Virginia Woolf and she had decided to pull the leg of dear old Ethel Smythe by pretending that they were lovers in front of her.

Irene now realized (the dogs emerging panting from spinney) that that conversation had taken place *after* the woman novelist had walked in the parks with Adriana, had talked in the restaurants with her, had read to her by her bedside and had finally decided, with so much reluctance, that she could not offer to be her Boswell.

Could it be, Irene now puzzled, that for once someone had succeeded in exploiting Adriana, instead of being exploited by her?

Unmaking

THERE were fourteen main bedrooms, each with a bathroom and each with a balcony that fringed the gleaming eyeball of the lake. There were two dining-rooms, one for when the Principessa was alone and one for when she was entertaining, a *salotto* and a *salottino*, a billiard-room, a ballroom, a music room, a library and a room, its walls covered in crimson damask, with nothing in it but four card tables, inlaid with mother-of-pearl and banded with brass, and the sixteen lyre-backed chairs that went with them. There were long, high-ceilinged passages, a labyrinth of them, with carpets, to which age had given a silvery patina, stretching down their centres. Each morning the thirty-two-year-old half-wit son of the Principessa's personal maid would push a carpet-sweeper, as though it were a toy horse, up and down them. From time to time, smiling or even giggling to himself, he would vary his usual sober pace with a sudden frenetic whoosh. There was no vacuum cleaner in the whole villa, just as there was no central heating, no wireless, no gramophone.

It was said that there were ten miles of walks in the grounds. Over the centuries this or that Principe or Principessa had thought, 'I'd like to see the view from that point' or 'It's a nuisance to have to walk round these rocks'; and at once *contadini* would be ordered to hack, hew and heave. Then someone would say, 'Oh, but the ladies must have a handrail' or 'Oh, but the old folk must have some steps'; and at once handrails were erected and steps were laid out. There were artificial grottoes, dripping moisure from what looked like artificial moss and ferns. There were tunnels and ruined towers, seldom entered because they were reputed to be the haunts of bats, and a number of 'dependencies' which housed poor relations, the bailiff and his family, estate workers, footmen and guests of whom the Principessa preferred not to see too much. Surmounting it all was a ruined chapel, dedicated to the Madonna of Montserrato; but after a landslide had obliterated the three young labourers who had been excavating yet another walk beneath it, it was now inaccessible except to the more adventurous of the children of the *contadini* who, finding a vertiginous foothold now here and now there among the boulders, would shin up to it as an act of bravado. Old Bruno, who had once been one of the three coachmen and was now one of the two chauffeurs, would shake his head and say that the chapel had become an evil place – *un posto cattivo*. But he never specified.

All these things, except the chapel and the remoter dependencies, the Principessa insisted on showing personally to the short, jolly, sweating German major and the tall, frigid, frowning lieutenant who accompanied him. '*La Principessa parla Tedesco?*' the major had inquired with an execrable accent. '*Disgraziatemente, non,*' she had answered, even though that was not true. '*Allora . . . ?*' The major did not feel equal to carrying on his negotiations in Italian. '*Inglese?*' suggested the lieutenant, who was examining a signed photograph of Queen Mary in a silver frame. 'Well, yes,' replied the Principessa with a little smile. 'Good,' said the major, who had once been a Rhodes scholar at Oxford. The lieutenant was now busy examining a signed photograph of the Duke of Aosta, also in a silver frame.

'I am not tiring you, Princess?' The major was solicitous, even though he had not guessed that this tall, erect, white-haired woman, with her smooth, rosy cheeks, her strong clear voice and her firm gait, had already passed her eightieth year.

'Not at all, thank you,' she answered.

As she opened one door after another – 'This is another bedroom', 'This used to be a nursery', 'This is only a box-room' – the major would advance straight to the tall windows, disregarding everything around him, would throw their halves open on to the narrow ledge of the balcony and would then step out, exclaiming, 'Beautiful!' or 'Magnificent!' or 'Splendid!' It was always left to the lieutenant to count the beds, to pull open drawers and to peer into the shadowy recesses of cupboards or of bathrooms in which huge old-fashioned bath tubs and bidets and throne-like water closets loomed up whitely. From time to time he would make some note on a sheet of paper attached to a clipboard.

In the lower, formal garden, the major snatched some lavender and, crushing it in his strong, stubby fingers, held it to his nose. 'What do you call this in English? I can't remember.' 'Lavender.' 'And in Italian?' 'Almost the same. *Lavanda.*' 'It sounds more beautiful in Italian. Everything is more beautiful in Italian.' From time to time he would stop, as so many of the villa guests had stopped before him, at some particularly breathtaking view of the lake or of the mountains and, like them, he would then exclaim, as on the balconies, 'Beautiful!' or 'Magnificent!' or 'Splendid!' Meanwhile the lieutenant, whistling under his breath, would scuff the gravel with one of his dusty boots or test the solidity of a handrail or the firmness of a flight of steps.

'Your family has lived here for a long time?'

'The Comadini have been here since the fifteenth century. It's thought that the original villa may have belonged to Pliny the Younger, as you probably know.' Of course the major knew nothing of the kind. 'There's a letter of his. He describes the villa as – let me remember – "supported by rock, as if by the buskins of the actors in tragedy" and goes on to say that he therefore calls it "Tragedia". His villa by the water he called "Commedia".' For the first time that afternoon the major ceased to smile. In their English versions he had no idea who Pliny the Younger was or what a buskin was.

'So much history,' he sighed.

'Yes, so much history,' she echoed with a flash of pride.

Later, in the *salottino*, seated in a straight-backed chair covered in a tooled Spanish leather, with the two officers enfolded (somehow to their disadvantage, each of them felt) in the embraces of two deep armchairs before and below her, the Principessa poured out tea from burnished silver into handleless cups of the finest porcelain. There was a faint smell of methylated spirit from the blue flame of the warmer; there was a faint smell of hay from the China tea. The 'cookies' – the Principessa used that word, not 'biscuits', when she offered them – were friable and lemony. They lay nestled in the folds of a heavy, lace-fringed napkin, which in turn rested on a silver dish.

'So what do you think of the villa?' she prompted with the faintest irony.

The major cleared his throat, reddening beneath his tan. 'Seldom have I seen . . . Indeed, never . . . Beautiful.' He heaved himself out of the armchair, as though out of a bath, and crossed to the window. The vast eyeball of the lake looked up at him; he looked down. 'This is very . . . distasteful,' he said. He meant it. He turned: 'In a war . . . and now that, in the South, the Italians . . . our former allies . . .'

'But of course. Let me give you some more tea.'

He shook his head with an odd, almost angry vehemence. 'Now that we are consolidating our position in this area, we need a house like this. For our headquarters.'

The Principessa nodded, her cup held between both her fragile hands. 'So you told me.'

'We shall take the utmost care. You may rely on that. The utmost care. Nothing will be damaged. We shall all be officers. We shall be' – again the blood rushed up under his tan, again he cleared his throat – 'most happy to employ all those whom you employ.'

The young lieutenant coolly put out a hand, took a sugar lump and placed it between his teeth. He began to suck, while still holding on to one end of it. The major and the Principessa both saw him but only the major was discomforted.

The major took two paces away from the open window and then two paces back to it. 'Of course you may stay on here,

Princess. There is no danger, none at all, that we should ask you to leave. But you understand – most of the rooms . . .'

'But of course!' He was relieved, if also puzzled, by her laughter.

'Your own suite of rooms. . . . There was, if I remember, a – a little study . . . ? Or perhaps we could spare you that little sitting-room. The – the . . . What did you call it?'

'The *salottino*.' The Principessa shook her head. 'No, I shall be quite happy in my own corner of the villa. Thank you all the same.'

'It would be difficult to offer you the music room – the piano. As you know, we Germans, like you Italians, love music. . . .'

'I never go into the music room now. Not since my husband's death.' She wondered what these Germans would have made of Guido, ceaselessly hammering out first ragtime and then jazz on the vast Bechstein grand that, because of the damp from the lake, was always in need of tuning.

'Ah, the Prince was musical!'

The Principessa gave her small, ironic smile. 'You might say that.'

The lieutenant glanced obtrusively at his watch and then tapped it with his forefinger, glancing over to his colleague. The major rose.

'On Monday afternoon – if that will suit you, of course, Princess – an advance party of us will come to make the final arrangements. Then on Tuesday . . .'

'You had better have a word with Franco.'

'Franco?'

'The majordomo. He'll look after you. But of course if there is more that I . . .'

'We shall try to make as little trouble as possible for you, Princess. No more than is absolutely necessary.'

In the long hall, hung with its murky portraits of centuries of Comadini – the Principessa had not accompanied them there – the major turned to the lieutenant. 'To have grown up in such a place!' he exclaimed in a tone of wonder.

The young lieutenant shrugged, drew a crumpled packet of cigarettes from a pocket of his tunic and stuck one in his mouth. He had been wanting to smoke throughout the visit and it baffled and annoyed him that he had not been able to bring himself to do so.

That evening, with the assistance of Franco, her personal maid, Ida, another maid and the lanky young footman who had been rejected for service because of his weak lungs, the Principessa moved into her suite of rooms all that she would require while the Germans were in residence. There were so many things of which she no longer made any use – the musty-smelling books in the library, the table of embroidery silks beside her high-backed chair in the *salottino*, ivory-topped walking sticks and parasols covered in brilliantly coloured satins, the baskets and leads and collars of dogs long dead and buried – but which she now felt an overwhelming sadness at abandoning, even if only temporarily. But when Franco, white-haired and distinguished as any ambassador, advised her that they must lock up or hide this or that, she gave a fatalistic shake of the head. 'We must trust them,' she said; and by that she meant 'We must trust Providence.' None the less, long after she had retired to bed, the old major-domo, the footman and the two maids busied themselves with packing up and transporting to cellars, outhouses and the empty dependencies scattered about the woodland everything that seemed to them to be particularly precious.

The old fear any change, however small, since it prefigures that greatest of all changes so near to them. But after that first overwhelming sadness, the Principessa felt strangely light-hearted as she took off her numerous rings and brooches and, with the assistance of the agitated maid, began to undress.

'Ah, Principessa, what a terrible thing to have happened!' Ida's hands trembled clumsily.

'Worse things are happening all over the world.'

Ida nodded. Her son, older brother of the half-wit, had been reported missing on the Russian front, just as the Principessa's only son had been reported missing at Caporetto so many years before.

'It'll all pass,' the Principessa said, slipping her arms into the sleeves of her silk nightdress with a small shudder of her ancient body.

'It'll all pass,' Ida repeated after her.

The Principessa lay in the dark, unable to sleep.

Her whole life, up to the moment when the two Germans had been announced to her, had been an infinitely laborious process of remaking. What had been ugly, crude, cheap, common, vulgar had, over a whole lifetime, been remade into the elegance, luxury, beauty, grandeur, distinction that this ancient villa symbolized. Few remembered it now but it was she who had bought back the whole estate: the villa itself from a Milanese industrialist on the point of bankruptcy; the dependencies from their humble inhabitants at grossly inflated prices; the strips of land from the *contadini* whose families had farmed them for generations. And it was she who had then put together all these separate fragments, like some skilled artisan mending, with infinite patience, a shattered work of art. Her husband, the Principe, had not cared for his lost patrimony. He was happy enough to live on her money in the Rome apartment in the Via Quattro Fontane, to play his bridge, to visit his mistress, to exercise his giant poodle, to go to nightclubs, to hammer out jazz on the piano. The Comadini name meant nothing to him; he was totally ignorant about the Comadini history. 'I am more Comadini than you,' she would tell him; and he knew that she was right and never contradicted her.

But the irony (of which only a few people were aware) was that she had not even been born Italian. Her mastery of the language, which she spoke so beautifully, was only another part of that whole laborious process of remaking – as was her acquisition of all the elaborately arcane forms and fashions of a class at first remote from her. She was like some upstart who seizes a throne and then rules with what seems to be an inherited finesse and assurance. Even some of the noblest of the nobility were a little in awe of her. She had so much more style, so much more authority and, most important of all, so much more money than themselves. That money, the black river on which all her gay, glittering, splendid edifices floated, had also been remade. Only a few people, most of them very old, were now able to trace it back to its source in America. Everyone else assumed that it was Comadini money, since there had been a long period when the Comadini had been some of the richest people in the world. Virtually no one knew of the Estonian Jew who had fled a pogrom in which his father and mother had been killed; who had arrived in Brooklyn with his ailing wife and infant daughter, unable to speak a word of the language of his country of adoption; and who had then, with a remarkable persistence, made a fortune from the garment industry, exploiting other emigrants less enterprising and ruthless than himself. There had eventually been a move from New York to New Jersey; and the child – to his grief his only one – had there been dispatched to Miss Dana's school in Morristown, where she mixed with the daughters of no less successful steel-makers, railroad tycoons, cattle barons, bankers and brokers. The unpronounceable Jewish surname was adapted into a pronounceable Gentile one.

Her mother by now had died, like some species no longer able to adjust to the ever-accelerating process of evolution. It was the girl's father who took her to London, Paris and Rome; and it was he who arranged for an eminent Swiss surgeon, long before the phrase 'plastic surgery' was known to the world, to break her nose brutally, as another stage, perhaps the most painful of all, in that whole lifelong process of remaking. (In later years people would often remark on the 'aristocratic distinction' of the Principessa's nose.) Then he set about marrying her off. There was an English baronet who all but took her and then decided not to – instead marrying, not one of his own kind, but, more humiliatingly, a Gaiety Girl. Next there was a Romanoff prince; but rumours, which the millionaire at first discounted, of a life of 'degeneracy' became too insistent. Finally, in Rome, the

last of the Comadini met, in both senses, his match. She had
always striven to placate and please her father, usually with no
success; but at last, shortly before his premature death from a
heart attack, she had succeeded in doing so by this most awe-
inspiring of dynastic alliances.

As she now reviewed this whole process of remaking, so
arduous that it sometimes seemed to her that she herself had
built the whole villa and laid out its gardens and woodlands with
her own bare hands, the Principessa now felt a tranquil satisfaction. Her head and shoulders propped up on pillows each of
the whitest and crispest Irish linen, with the princely monogram
stiff in a corner, she smiled into the darkness. Even that plump,
sweating major had not supposed for one second that she was
anything other than what the world had for so long accepted
her as being: Italian; Gentile; aristocratic. 'It'll all pass'; but what
she had remade, first at the command of her father, then at his
prompting and finally as a propitiary gesture to his shade, would
not pass. This riff-raff might briefly occupy the villa, their boots
trampling noisily up and down its corridors, their jeeps grinding
noisily up and down its drives, their harsh, guttural voices
echoing noisily up and down its stairwells. But it was *they* who
would pass.

Carlo had always been something of a fool; it never ceased to
amaze the Principessa that he had finally succeeded in getting
where he was. When his father, like her son, had been killed in
the First World War, she had taken his mother into service as a
laundrywoman and had allowed her and the baby to establish
themselves in three cramped, low-raftered rooms under the roof
of the villa. Instead of playing rough, noisy games with the
other children on the estate, Carlo, a sickly boy with pitifully
thin arms and legs and an overlarge head perpetually tipped to
one side as though it were too heavy for the support of his neck,
would follow his mother everywhere with a lamblike bleating of
'Mamma! Mamma! Mamma!' He was later teased and bullied
at the local school for his inability to master even such elementary

skills as throwing a ball overarm, riding a bicycle or flirting with a girl. Later still, when he worked briefly in the villa as a footman, his sleepy, faintly insolent inefficiency got on the Principessa's nerves. Eventually, his mother dead, he left the villa and the village first for Milan and then for Rome. And now here he was, back as the Fascist boss of the area.

Since his return, he had made it a habit to call from time to time on the Principessa, his dark suit or his uniform well pressed, his shoes or boots gleaming and his nails manicured to a pinkish gloss. He had acquired weight, both of body and of authority; in his sallow, hook-nosed, narrow-browed way he had even grown handsome. In the winter the two of them would sit before the log fire, drinking the China tea that smelled of hay; in the summer they would sit out on the terrace, he with a Campari soda and she with a fresh orange juice in a slender glass pearled with moisture from the ice cubes in it. There was still deference in his treatment of her; but the deference was that of a man to a woman, of someone young to someone old, and not of an inferior to a superior.

When the footman had placed the silver tea service before the Principessa – because of the imminent arrival of the Germans, they were meeting for the first time in her boudoir – Carlo rose, tiptoed to the door and made sure that it was shut. Really, thought the Principessa, despite all outward changes he's remained as essentially silly as he always was.

'I'm horrified by this news.'

'Why? What's happened now?' She was thinking of the armies pushing up inexorably through the south of Italy.

'The villa, the Germans.' He spoke in a hoarse undertone, as though behind one of the tapestries or inside one of her cupboards some German eavesdropper might be lurking.

'Oh that!' She picked up one of the friable, lemon-flavoured 'cookies' and bit into it. 'Oh, I'll survive that. After all, I've survived a great deal in a long life. Those that I've so far met seem pleasant enough. The Germans are usually, well, correct, if nothing else. Aren't they?'

He shook his head gloomily; and she remembered, for a brief irrelevant moment, that child's head lolling to one side and that baa-like 'Mamma! Mamma! Mamma!'

'After all, what can they do to harm an old woman like me? I'll hide away in these quarters here until the time comes for them to move on. It can't be long now,' she all but added and then checked herself, remembering who this new Carlo was.

'Principessa, you could be in danger.'

'Danger!'

'I oughtn't to be saying this to you. If they knew in Milan or if the Germans here knew . . . But I owe you a debt. A great debt. And I've not forgotten it. Never.' Emotion made his voice swell and tremble.

'Debt? What do you mean, Carlo?'

He looked affronted and aggrieved, not realizing that she had been kind to so many dependants of the villa not out of any spontaneous impulse but merely out of obedience to the Comadini code. But then he told himself that she was old, old, and that her memory was probably failing. Patiently he reminded her of what she needed no reminding: 'You took us in, my mother and me. After my father's death. You paid for my mother's funeral. For my education.'

'Oh that! But that was nothing!' She was totally unaware of her cruelty.

He leant towards her, brown hands clasped tightly in each other. The light from the lamp beside him – the heavy lace curtains of the boudoir excluded almost all the daylight – gleamed on those square fingernails buffed to an opalescent pink.

'You're in danger, Principessa. I know what I'm talking about.'

'Oh, don't be so silly!'

But he persisted: 'In the past – before the Germans came – there were rumours about you. About your ancestry. And so on. But it was easy for me, in my position . . . '

'What rumours?' She imagined the sleepy, faintly insolent young footman grubbing about among her papers; forcing locked drawers to do so; listening at doors when she spoke to her lawyer from Milan or her financial adviser from New York.

He faltered, hardly daring to put the rumours into words.

'Well?' she demanded.

'You are, of course – were, of course – American. We're at war with America, Principessa. I don't have to tell you that.'

'I've been an Italian for many, many years. For more years than you have lived. My only son died for Italy at Caporetto.'

He inclined his head, with a sigh. 'Still . . .' He began to tinkle the spoon round and round the cup on the spindly table before him. The Principessa felt an urge to put out a hand to stop the ceaseless movement. He had always had the knack of getting on her nerves. Then he went on in a hoarse whisper totally unlike his usual firm, commanding tone: 'There's the other matter, too, of course.'

'The other matter?'

'These rumours . . . rumours . . .'

'Yes?'

'Well – about – about your race, Principessa.' He could not bring himself to say 'Jewish' or 'Jew'.

'Oh.' She sucked in her cheeks, so that the smooth, rosy cheekbones suddenly became more prominent and the lips were bunched into an ugly knot. So the sleepy, faintly insolent foot-man had been more observant than she had ever imagined possible. 'I see.'

'To me of course all that's nothing. Of no importance at all. To most of us Italians, as you know. . . . But these Germans . . .'

She stared at him with a kind of inquiring disdain: Who are you? What are you? What are you doing here in my house and my boudoir? He wriggled in the constriction of his dark suit, putting two fingers inside his stiff collar.

She gave a little snort at the back of the 'distinguished' nose which, more than half a century before, that eminent Swiss surgeon had brutally smashed with a little hammer. 'What can they do to me?' she demanded. 'Whatever I may or may not be.' She was, he saw, going to admit nothing.

Resentment at her ingratitude and contempt suddenly swelled in him. 'There are Camps. You must have heard of them. Even people as distinguished as yourself, as rich as yourself . . .' (He almost went on, 'As old as yourself.') 'They have no pity. None at all. Believe me.'

'Oh, my dear Carlo . . . !' It was the same tone, contemptuously amused, that she had used when her dead husband had confessed some new folly to her – an unpaid tailor's bill, the purchase or crashing of yet another sports car, the acquisition or ditching of yet another mistress. She put down her cup and, picking up the small, lace-edged linen square in her lap, she dabbed at her lips with it.

'I'm being very serious, Principessa. Your situation could be very grave indeed.'

'Nonsense!' She was getting to her feet; she was taller than he, even when he too rose and faced her. 'Anyway – what do you imagine that I can do about it?'

'You must get away. As soon as possible.'

She stared at him, incredulous.

'Yes!' His was now the insistence of a parent to a disobedient child. 'You've no time to lose.'

'Oh, really, Carlo! Do you expect me to leave my villa, my village, my people, my whole life here . . . ? You must be crazy! At my age? Do you realize that I'm eighty-three?'

'Principessa – please go! While you still have a chance. I'll see to it' – again his voice assumed that conspiratorial whisper – 'that no one stops you. You could slip over the mountains to Switzerland. Others have done it, you know that. Or the lake . . . But once the Germans are settled in . . .'

She gazed at him with exactly the same expression – unimpressed, pitying, sardonic – with which she used to receive his or his mother's tales of how the other children on the estate had been bullying him. Then she shook her head. 'It's out of the question. Quite out of the question. And I'm sure not even necessary. But thank you, Carlo – thank you all the same.'

After he had gone, his face flushed with chagrin, she thought

cynically to herself: He's afraid, that one. He always was afraid.
A coward. A mean little coward. He knows the war is ending. He
already sees himself hung up by the heels in the market square. He
wants to earn some credit with me and with every other
decent person.

It was a squat closed van, such as might be used to transport a
cow to the bull or a pig to the slaughter-house. The tyres were
thick, their treads worn, and the black paint was pocked and
scored. Looking down at it from above, she thought: It might
be a hearse. Ida stood fearfully beside her, her eyes raw from
weeping.

There was a knock at the door of the boudoir and the German
major, sweating even more than usual, was outside. He clicked
his heels and bowed. 'We are ready, Principessa,' he said in a
small humbled voice.

'I really can't see why Bruno shouldn't drive me in one of the
two cars – instead of having to travel in *that*.'

'I'm sorry, Principessa.' He genuinely was sorry. 'Shall we go?'

She pointed to a small, crocodile-leather suitcase, surprisingly
heavy because of its silver fittings. Many years ago her husband
had shot the crocodile. It was almost as though she expected the
major to carry it; but from behind him a private soldier, with a
soft doughy face and hair the colour of lard, stepped forward.
She heard the scrape of his hobnailed boots on the elaborate
parquet but it meant nothing to her, as once it would have done.
Ida gave a little sob.

On the wide staircase the major leant towards her. 'You
understand, don't you, Principessa? All this is nothing to do
with me. But soon you will be back. This evening. Tomorrow
at the latest. Just a simple interrogation. There has been some
mistake.'

She could see faces at the windows round the courtyard: some,
frightened or grief-stricken, of the servants; more, inquisitive or
apathetic, of the Germans. She raised a valedictory hand to the
servants and nodded, now in this direction and now in that.

'I shall see you this evening,' the major said, as though to
reassure himself, rather than her. 'Or tomorrow.'

She shook his hand, feeling it pulse oddly, as though it were
an imprisoned bird, in her firm grasp. 'Thank you.' She knew
that this silly, anxious man meant well.

He helped her up into the van and then, taking the old-
fashioned crocodile-leather suitcase, with its faded gold monogram, from the soldier, handed that in too. There were two
soldiers inside, at either end of a hard bench. She sat on another
hard bench opposite to them. She did not mind the hardness;
she had always chosen upright chairs without upholstery. For a
brief moment she glimpsed Ida's face, convulsed by grief and
terror, behind the major's shoulder; she heard a long animal
wail, like the wail that her beloved saluki dog used to give when
she went out and left him behind her. Then the doors of the van
crashed shut and someone outside drew across the bolts.

The two soldiers opposite stared down at their clumsy boots,
deliberately avoiding her calm, candid gaze. The van began to
throb; then, with a crunch of gravel, it swayed round in a circle
and began to move forward.

She could see nothing now but the two soldiers, a squashed
cigarette butt between the feet of one of them and, high above
their heads, a patch of moving, changing green, criss-crossed by
wire netting. But she knew the winding drive so well that at no
moment was she in any ignorance of her whereabouts. Now they
had taken the hairpin bend where, last year, torrential rain had
brought a boulder thundering down; now they were passing
the little chapel, with its elaborate stucco work and its Luini, too
soft and sentimental for her taste, of a Mother and Child; and
now that sudden lurch of the van to the left must mean that they
had swerved to avoid the wood piled there from the fallen
chestnut tree. Finally they were making the detour round the
kitchen gardens to pass the row of *contadini* dwellings. She
wondered if any of the *contadini* were watching the van as it
passed; she wondered how many of them regretted its passing.

She had felt a stoical calm and patience till this moment; but as the van turned out from the drive on to the main road, gravel giving way to smoother asphalt, she was surprised by a sudden access of joy, as though the thin, sluggish blood in her eighty-three-year-old body had suddenly started to flow more copiously and faster through her narrowing arteries. All that she had remade, so laboriously and at so much cost, through more than half a century, denying all the deepest needs of her nature, had in a single week been unmade again; and though the stones of the villa might still go on standing – as a hotel, as a hostel, as a rest home, as a conference centre – it too had been unmade as effectively as if those Germans had exploded a bomb in it.

But, strangely, she felt no grief or rage or fear but only this exhilaration. Almost a century before some obscure Estonians had been driven out of their burning hovels; and now she, bearer of one of the most distinguished names in the whole world, was being driven out of a palace contaminated by alien presences. The thread, winding back from the vast estate on the promontory to the little village in the marshes, so long ago and so brutally and so decisively severed, had now been knit together again. She could feel it all in her hands, a complete, integral spool. She smiled across at the guards, who at once looked away.

Love's Old Sweet Song

I

TONY sat there, silent.

Hans said in his heavy German–American accent (we were at a party): 'How did we meet? Well, Tony ought really to tell you that because he's so much funnier when he tells a story than I ever am. But I was passing Harrods and I thought, "Hell, it's time I got myself half-a-dozen neckties and there, at the necktie counter, was this perfectly gorgeous blond. Well, you can see for yourself! He's really an actor, you know, but actors don't work in England these days unless they're working at necktie counters or places like that. Well, I picked out this necktie, it was designed by your Hardy Amies, a really beautiful design, and I held it against my shirt and I asked him, "Well, how does it suit me?" And the son-of-a-bitch said, cool as a cucumber, with that lovely British drawl of his, "It would suit me but it doesn't suit you. You're too old for it." Well, I just love that kind of sassiness, I thought it just great. So I said, "OK, kid, I'll buy it for you. But only on one condition. That you wear it to a party that I'm going to next Saturday. And he said, "Is it going to be a gay party?" and I put on this very, *very* British accent, just to take the mickey out of him as you say over here, and I replied, "Yes, madly gay, darling. You can bet your cute little ass on that." So here we both are.'

2

Tony stood there, silent.

Hans said in his heavy German–American accent (we had met

in a Notting Hill Gate pub): 'Yep, he's left Harrods. As you
know, I'm an acquisitive sort of bastard and when I see something I like, then I go out and get it. He's more decorative than
that Tiffany lamp of mine. Better value than that hideous
Victorian *cache-pot* that you talked me into buying at that
auction sale in Worthing. Much, much more comforting to wake
up to than my Francis Bacon Pope in his glass box. *And* he can
cook! Boy, can he cook! Yesterday we had these *polpettini*
things – a superior kind of meatball you might call them, but
out of this world, just out of this world. And today we had this
chicken dish with the creamiest of creamy white sauces and
asparagus and . . . Well, *he* should really be telling you all about
this, not me. . . . He's such terrific company, that's what I really
like about him, the bed thing apart. Until you really know him,
you don't know how witty he can be. When he was still at
Harrods, this nasty old buzzard, the floor manager or something,
came over and wanted to know why he hadn't done what he'd
been told to do and got his neckties into order. And Tony drew
himself up to his full five foot six and said with the most withering
scorn you can imagine, 'I've been too fucking busy. Or vice
versa." Got it? Or *vice versa*. Well, I suppose if he'd been too
busy fucking, I had to carry the can for that. So I said to him,
"Tony, you don't have to eat that kind of shit. There are better
things in life for you than selling neckties."'

3

Tony ate there, silent.

Hans said in his heavy German–American accent (we were at
his lunch table): 'Yep, the garden's never looked better. This
boy of mine has green fingers all right. He knew nothing about
roses, not a thing, and when he started pruning them, old
O'Leary, he's the Irish drunk who comes by when it suits him to
potter around the garden and take a fiver for it, well, he all but
hit the ceiling. But those roses have done better than they've
ever done before, we've had so many blooms that right after

lunch Tony's going to go out and pick you a whole bunch of
them to take home with you, because I know that in that little
yard of yours it's difficult for you to get anything to grow at all.
. . . This'll interest you, it's really our secret, Tony's and mine,
but Tony won't mind my telling you, since he knows that
you're one of my oldest and dearest friends. Tony's working on
this novel, so far he's done only two or three pages, but they're
brilliant. I mean that, *brilliant.* He's a natural and I don't have to
tell you that a natural's a truly rare thing. When he's done that
first chapter, I'm going to make him let you have a peek at it,
because you'll understand at once what a privilege that is. He's
such a modest kid, I'll know I'll have to force him, but you're
going to agree with me, you're going to see that he has a real,
real potential. Christ, he doesn't seem to have to work to get his
effects as most of you writers have to. Mind you, he finds it
difficult to get settled to his desk in London. Too many dis-
tractions and I don't just mean the Coleherne. So we've been
looking at country cottages and we think, we *think,* keep your
fingers crossed, that we've found just the thing to suit us. Four
beds, three baths. This big, big sitting-room, a dining-room, a
kind of music room and this study for Tony boy. It's a beautiful
little place, real period, Tudor or Jacobean, I never know the
difference, and Tony's going to be the most beautiful thing in it,
you can bet your life on that. Oh, and it has the funniest name.
Fog End. I looked at that name on the gate and Tony looked at
that name on the gate and then he said, quick as lightning,
because you know how quick he is, 'We'll have to change that
O to an A." Got it? Not Fog End. *Fag* End. So I decided to
play it cool and I replied, "Well, yes, Tony, I do smoke too
much." But wasn't that just marvellous? That's what I just
love about Tony, that surprising kind of wit.'

4

Tony walked there, silent.
Hans said in his heavy German–American accent (we were on

the downs near the cottage): 'Now you're not going to be offended if Tony takes off after tea, are you? This kind of country life is fine for us middle-aged folk but someone of Tony's age wants to be right in there in the thick of things. He wants to see this new production at Covent Garden, he's just crazy about Caballe. You ought to hear him sing himself. He's got this really lovely light tenor voice, something like Luigi Alva. I keep telling him that he ought to have it trained. But he says, "For me it would have to be Brünnhilde or nothing and I haven't the size for her." Now isn't that the funniest thing you ever heard? Yes, you must get Tony to talk about music to you. He's so *knowledgeable*, I mean he can reel off to you every damn recording by his beloved Caballe or Callas or Sutherland. . . . Is he taking the train? Oh, no, no, not our Tony! We now have the most beautiful, not to say the most expensive, Yamaha motorcycle and the most beautiful, not to say the most expensive, leather jacket and pants and boots to go with it. And lots and *lots* of chains of course! All that equipment practically bankrupted me. But who cares? Just so long as my Tony is happy. And besides, now that he has a motorcycle of his own, we're saving money on all that gas for the Volvo.'

5

Tony was not there.

Hans said in his heavy German–American accent (he was sitting opposite me in my house): 'I couldn't tell anyone but you this, because I wouldn't want to do Tony dirt, whatever he's done to me, but that first time, when he got undressed and I saw those underpants of his lying on the floor and then I saw those feet . . . If someone who doesn't *have* to be dirty – someone who has every chance to be clean – lets himself go like that, well, it somehow makes you worry. I was always having to nag at him, "Now, Tony, we've got company coming, please, *please* take a bath or a shower." . . . Yep, I suppose he *was* good-looking in that rather slope-shouldered, wide-hipped way of his. But, boy, was he dumb! Well, you saw for yourself. He'd

sit over on that chair of yours over there or he'd be sitting in
the best armchair back at my place or he'd be standing with his
drink at a pub or a club and he just made no effort, he never said
a single goddamn word. Well, you saw for yourself! You'd often
try to draw him out, I'll say that for you, you sweated blood,
but who was it who answered you, who always had to answer
you? Tell me that!

'. . . But you know, it was those little dishonesties that I
couldn't really take, because I am, as you know, a basically very,
very honest person myself. I mean, once we came here, I
remember, and you went out of the room to get some ice, it was
one of those days when by some miracle you happened to have
some, and he picked up this cigar box here of yours, this box of
lousy Panatellas, and he calmly, just like that, put two or three in
his pocket. I'd have told him to put them right back but at that
moment you came back in again, bearing two or three of those
darling little ice cubes of yours as though they were diamonds,
and I just felt too fucking embarrassed to say anything in front
of you. He'd help himself to bills from my wallet without a by-
your-leave. Did you know that? Yes, I'm not making this up!
And since he's gone, I've found all kinds of small things missing.
Those cufflinks that Darlene gave me, remember? I never liked
them, I know they were trash, but still I never expected him to
steal them from me.

'. . . Of course my great mistake, I see it now, was to buy him
all that gear. But it was nag, nag, nag morning, noon and night
and you know how damn persistent he could be when he'd
set his little heart on something. Once he'd got that motorcycle,
it was all he ever thought about. And then in no time at all he was
in with that leather crowd. And you know what *that* means.
Many's the time he'd come home black and blue. Or worse.

'. . . Of course it was crazy of me to believe all that crap about
his great, *great* love of music and how he must hear Caballe or
Sutherland or some other of those peahens screeching her head
off. Because, as I've since discovered, he was really spending
those times away on a series, a whole squalid series, of one-night

stands. That kid could just never get enough! . . . Well, of course, since you ask, I *do* miss him from time to time. But, boy, is it nice to no longer have to worry about crabs or clap or even worse! And it's even nicer not to have to listen to that endless yackety-yackety-yak. Talk about verbal diarrhoea! Tony's was a case of verbal amoebic dysentery. There were all these intelligent, well-informed people, people with experience, people like ourselves, but would he keep that big mouth of his shut for a moment? No, sir! . . . What's he doing now? Who cares? He'll always land on somebody's feet, if not on his own.'

6

Bobby sat there, silent.

Hans said in his heavy German–American accent (we were again at a party): 'What I like about Bobby here is that he's just one hundred per cent reliable. Well, I know that he has all other kinds of assets, both visible and invisible as the economists say, but that's the one I value most. That and this fantastic wit of his. When we first met – it was in Fortnum's and I was ordering that candy that I sent to you in hospital – and I said to him, "Look, a good friend of mine was going to accompany me to the theatre this evening but now he's sick in hospital and so why don't you come with me instead?" And he looked me up and down in that cool, elegant way of his, very British, and then he said with that lovely British drawl of his, "Why not? I need a good fairy to look after me." Now wasn't that just perfect? I laugh whenever I remember it.

'. . . Tony? *Tony?* Now fancy your remembering Tony. Haven't you heard? He's dead. Yes, sugar, dead. D–E–A–D. . . . How did he die? Well, his mother said that it was some kind of perforated ulcer but that's the kind of crap that mothers are fed by doctors, isn't it? My own view is that it was the hard stuff. It had to be. . . . An alcoholic? No, sugar, the hard stuff – heroin. . . . Well, of course he was on it! Sometimes you novelists do manage to be incredibly unobservant and naive. I knew it at once, that first time we went to bed together. He had these horrible sores all up his arms. It quite turned me off, you know how squeamish I am. The needle . . . You never saw any? Sugar, it's time you got yourself some new bifocals. . . . *Of course* he was hooked. That's why he was always taking money from my wallet and grabbing things to hock. Yeah, poor kid, he had it coming to him. Yeah . . . You know, sometimes, sometimes, I wake up in the night, with this cute little trick snoring beside me, and somehow, somehow, remembering our times together, I just can't believe, just can't believe at all that that little mother-fucker is really and truly dead.'

The Stepson's Story

WHATEVER I may have imagined at the time and have sometimes imagined since, surely Pop couldn't really have aimed at
me? (I call him Pop because that's what he's always wanted me
to call him and because that's what Laura, my half-sister, has
always called him. He's my American stepfather, an army
major who deals with catering, and he's been married for so
long to my mother that I don't really remember anyone else,
even though my mother often says, 'Of *course* you remember
Daddy,' as though she were somehow trying to force me to do
so.) I mean, why should Pop have aimed at me instead of at the
man? It doesn't make any sense. He admitted in court that he was
so angry and excited and confused that he had no real idea of
what he was doing – 'Everything just went red' was how he
described it. And, in any case, he had never had any practice in
firing a gun for years – not since he first joined the Army. No,
he couldn't have aimed at me. I must have imagined it; that first
shot must just have gone astray.

It all happened in Holland Park more than a year ago, but I
still often think about it, here in San Diego, just as I still often
think about St Paul's and my English friends and our London
flat. I used to love that park; it seemed to be so much larger than
it really was, parts of it almost like a wood in the country. I never
in the least minded taking the dog for a walk in it, even when it
was raining and no one else wanted to take him. But now
nothing would persuade me to go into it ever again. Sometimes
I even still have nightmares about it – about that low wall and
the tree with the fork in it and the rain dripping off the leaves of
the tree and then those two shots. I never talk about the night-

mares to Pop, because I know he wouldn't like it, and when I mention them to Mother she looks somehow worried and sad at one and the same time, and then she tells me that it's all in the past now, I must put it out of my mind and forget all about it. But it's not easy to do that. I wonder if I'll ever be able to do that.

In spite of the man I think that we were happier that summer than we'd ever been before – and, I sometimes think, than we'll ever be again. I don't like to say that, because most of the time Pop wasn't with us and it seems strange to have been so happy when, except for two or three days here and there, it was just the three of us together. Although we never admitted it to each other, and although I don't care to admit it even now, I think that we all rather dreaded Pop's returns to us from Scotland. We were so cosy together, the three of us, so cosy and comfortable. We had meals when we wanted them and we often didn't eat at home but at the new Macdonald's or at the cafeteria of the Commonwealth Institute. We didn't bother about keeping the flat too tidy, and Laura and I went to bed, not at nine as we did when Pop was around, but at any hour we felt like. Mother would return from the telephone and say something like 'Pop will be with us on Friday; now, isn't that marvellous?' or 'Children, it's good news! We'll be having Pop home tomorrow,' but I felt – I don't know why – that she was never really as pleased and excited as she wanted us to think she was. Then we'd also pretend to be more pleased and excited than we really were. Laura would overdo it even more than I did, and I would then understand what Aunt Amy, mother's older sister, meant when she described her, more than once, as 'quite the little actress'. 'Oh, Mother!' she'd squeal in the same piercing voice that she now uses when she's talking to one of her boy-friends on the telephone. 'Oh, that's terrific! Oh, I can't believe it! Pop home again!'

Laura was very proud, even while we were still living in England, of being an American and speaking with an American accent just like Pop's. I was equally proud of being English and speaking with an English accent just like Mother's. Pop often makes fun of what he calls my 'British' or 'limey' way of talking. If, for example, at table I say, 'Could you please pass the salt?' he answers, 'Certainly, old chap! I'll be only too delighted to *pahss* anything you wish to you.' Sometimes, instead of 'old chap' he calls me 'Sir Laurence' meaning Laurence Olivier. I notice that he never makes fun of Mother's accent, even though it's exactly the same as mine. Once or twice I've said to Mother that I'm sick of Pop going on and on about the way I speak – after all, I *am* English, aren't I? But each time she's answered that I must learn not to be so sensitive, Pop likes his little joke, he just teases me out of friendliness and affection.

When Pop arrived from Scotland, he always seemed to be tired and vaguely worried. His catarrh was bad, he would complain; or he had his old back trouble; or he wished that he could get rid of this goddamn headache. Mother would ask him why on earth he didn't take a sleeper instead of driving through the night; and then he would either say that the journey was cheaper by car and *she* ought to know how badly we needed to cut down on expenses or else that, driving alone like that for hour after hour, he found he could unwind. But he never seemed to be unwound by the time that he reached us. Just the opposite. Over breakfast he would either sit silent, staring ahead of him as he chewed and swallowed, chewed and swallowed, and gulped down coffee so hot that it made his nose go red, or else he would tell Mother about his boss, the Colonel – 'that goddamn bastard!' he would often call him – and about his rows with him and about what he was going to say to him next time he handed him the same sort of shit. I had the feeling that, face to face with his boss, he always accepted the shit and said nothing at all.

Pop would go to bed after breakfast and Laura and I, if we were not at school, and if we did not want to go out, would then have to be very, very quiet. We couldn't play the hi-fi or talk except in whispers, we had to be careful not to bang the doors and we were not supposed to pull the chain or run the taps. If we forgot any of these things, we'd hear Pop groaning from the bedroom at the end of the passage, 'Oh, for Christ's sake!' and then Mother would hurry in to us and whisper that we must be more considerate, Pop was very, *very* tired.

By the time that lunch was over, he had usually recovered and I began to think that he was really a very nice stepfather to have, if one couldn't have a real father. Sometimes, it's true, he'd criticize Mother for the state of the kitchen or say that he could have eaten a better meal in the mess any day; or he'd go into my room or Laura's room and shout out, 'Do you have to live in this kind of pigsty? Here, get this place straight! Pronto!' He'd stand over us after that, hands on hips, watching us through narrowed eyes as we tidied things up. Then, all at once he'd become jolly and friendly. 'That's my girl!' he'd say or 'That's my boy!' and he'd hug Laura or put an arm around my shoulders and then he'd suggest that maybe we'd like to go with him to this or that museum or this or that movie. We preferred the movies to the museums but we never told him that. He loves old things even though, as he often tells us, he's never been able to afford to collect them because of all his 'family obligations'. In the Victoria and Albert Museum or the British Museum he would sometimes stand for minutes on end before a showcase, watching some piece of jewellery from one of those Egyptian tombs or some piece of gold or silver from one of those Greek burial mounds as though he expected it to move. Sometimes he would take us rowing on the Serpentine or to the Zoo or to the Planetarium or some place like that. It was fun to be with him then. I don't want to suggest that he was always silent or bad-tempered. He could be great fun, laughing and joking and mimicking people so well that it was almost uncanny to hear him.

Laura and I were much closer that summer than we had ever been before, even though we went to different schools and even though, at fifteen, I thought of myself as almost grown-up and I thought of her, four years younger, as still a child. But I sometimes got the idea that Pop didn't like us to be *too* friendly. When he wasn't there, we'd got into the habit of my going into her bedroom at night, after we'd undressed, and lying on her bed and chatting to her. When Pop learned about that, he said at once that it had to stop. I was surprised that something so unimportant should have made him so angry not only with me but also with Mother. He went quite pale and the sweat broke out on his forehead, as it always does when he loses his temper, while he told us, all three of us, not once but two or three times, that he wasn't going to have it. 'Haven't you any sense of responsibility? Are you out of your mind?' he shouted at Mother. 'How can I feel at ease up there in Scotland, when I just don't know what you're allowing to go on down here?' Mother kept calm, as she almost always does, and did not even pause in her knitting. Later, when she came to say goodnight to me, I whispered, 'He oughtn't to talk to you like that. I hate it when he does it.' She shrugged, as she stooped to put out the lamp beside my bed. Then out of the darkness I heard her: 'He's been very good to us. You mustn't forget that. Given us a lovely home. Made it possible for you to go to St Paul's instead of to a comprehensive. He flies off the handle but he doesn't really mean it. He has so much on his mind.'

Another time he found a magazine among the papers on my desk. He was looking for a rubber and then all at once, as I was watching 'Panorama' on the telly, I heard him shouting to me to go to him at once – pronto! 'Where did you get this filth?' he demanded, his face pale and those beads of sweat on his forehead. I told him that a boy at school had lent me the magazine – which was the truth. 'I won't have this kind of thing in the house! I don't give a damn what you read at school or in the park or anywhere else. But I won't have it here. Do you understand?' He began to try to tear it up, his previously pale face now turning red as he tugged at the pages. One or two pieces fell to the floor and then, stooping to pick them up, he said in a breathless voice, 'I'll have to burn it.' But before doing that he went on again: 'I will not have this kind of filth in this house. Laura might come in here and see it. She might pick it up and not know what it was. I can't have her mind exposed to that kind of – that kind of — '

I waited for the word 'filth' and the word 'filth' came sure
enough. Later I wondered why I had been so foolish as to leave
that magazine out on my desk, when usually I hid such things
under the bed or beneath a pile of clothes in my chest of drawers.
It was almost as though I had *wanted* him to come on it.

Of course, since she's his very own daughter and I'm only
some other man's son, Pop has always loved Laura more than
me. That's only natural; it would be odd if he didn't. But he
would get equally angry with both of us in those London days
and he was usually far stricter with Laura than with me – which
is saying a lot! All the same, I always knew that Laura was the
favourite. When she was doing her homework at one end of the
table in the sitting-room and I was doing mine at the other end,
he would lean over her, his body against hers and a hand on her
shoulder, as he looked over what she had done or told her what
to do. Sometimes he would lift up a handful of the blonde hair
that fell across her face – not so much, it always seemed, so that
she could see her work better but so that he could see her better.
When we all watched the telly – he liked the programmes about
exploration and travels to foreign countries and new scientific
discoveries, while Laura and I would have preferred 'Kojak' or
'Columbo' or something like that – he would call across to
Laura, 'Isn't my little girl going to come to sit on Pop's knee?'
and Laura would then sometimes go over and do what he said
and sometimes answer in a surprisingly cross and impatient
voice that it was far too hot to sit so close to another person or
that she could see better where she was. He would bring us all
presents from Scotland but, while to Mother or me he would say
something like 'I've brought this for you' or 'You may find this
useful', to Laura he would say something like 'Would my
beautiful daughter like to see the lovely surprise that I've got
for her?' Once he brought her a little Victorian locket shaped
like a heart with a small ruby in the middle of it – it must have
cost him a lot – and he himself put it around her neck, lifting up
the fair hair to fasten the clasp at the back, and then he put his
hands on her shoulders, looked at her and bent down and kissed

her on the forehead. Of course, no father would kiss his son like that; but I couldn't help wishing that once, just once, he had looked at me with that kind of affection and tenderness.

Laura first saw the man when we were taking the spaniel, Benny, for a walk in Holland Park. We had decided to separate from each other for a little, because I wanted to watch the tennis and she wanted to go down to the playground to see if any of her school-friends were there. But then, within three or four minutes, there she was, back again. She didn't say anything, she just came and stood beside me, but as she stooped to pat the dog, I noticed that her eyes seemed to be opened more widely than usual and that her face was like Pop's when he was angry, all white and sweaty.

'Didn't you go to the playground?'

She swallowed in an odd way, as though on something bitter, and then shook her head.

'Why not?'

Still she did not speak but just shrugged her shoulders. Her lower lip was trembling now.

Soon after that we left the tennis and began to walk home. It was then that she said, 'I saw something. Something very peculiar happened to me just now.'

I asked her what, but she just shook her head.

'Go on, tell me! Don't be such an ass!'

Again she shook her head. But at last I got it out of her. 'There was this – this man. In a long grey raincoat. And a strange cap. And he looked at me in such a funny way and then he . . . he . . .' She broke off.

'Yes?' I said.

Suddenly she began to laugh and then the laughter turned to crying.

'Well?' I said. 'What was it? What did he do? What's the matter with you?' That strange laughter-crying had begun to frighten me a little.

'He – he . . . His – his *thing* was out!'

'What?'

'His – his *thing*!'

'Is *that* all?' I began to laugh and then the crying part of what she was doing stopped all of a sudden and she was laughing, too.

'It looked so odd,' she said. 'Weird. A kind of purple colour. And so big. It – it kind of frightened me.'

'Dirty old man!' I said, still laughing at the picture. 'You don't want to let a dirty old man like that upset you.' And 'Dirty old man!' she repeated, also still laughing.

I thought no more about it. But the next day Laura told a friend at school, a girl I never really liked, and the girl told her mother. The result was that Mrs Bacon (as she was called) telephoned to Mother and then came round. It was Laura who happened to answer the bell and, having told Mother who it was, she then rushed in to me. At the time neither of us knew about Mrs Bacon's telephone call. 'Oh Lord! Oh gosh! Oh heavens!' She put her hands up to her cheeks and swayed from side to side, as she still does when she's embarrassed or upset.

'What is it?'

'It's Mrs Bacon.'

'And who's she?'

'Angela's mother.'

'What's she come about?' I was wishing that Laura would leave me alone to get on with a watch I was trying to repair.

Laura did not reply. Instead she threw herself face downwards on my bed, still saying 'Oh Lord! Oh gosh! Oh heavens!' and things like that and wriggling about like a fish that's just been hooked. I got up and went into the sitting-room to have a peep at this Mrs Bacon.

The two of them stopped talking as I appeared. Mrs Bacon – who, I later learned, was some kind of social worker – had fat arms and legs and a large bosom that jutted out, quite close to her chin, like a shelf. Her face, under a bright-red hat shaped like a coal-scuttle, looked hot and no less red. 'What do you want, dear?' Mother asked and, before I had time to answer, went on: 'This is my son.'

'Oh, yes, I've heard about him,' Mrs Bacon said in a voice that suggested that all she had heard might not be good.

'I was looking for my trigonometry book,' I said after I had shaken her hand. The hand seemed strangely cold in contrast to the hotness of her face.

'It doesn't seem to be here,' Mother said, looking vaguely around her. 'Now, could you leave us alone for a little, there's a dear? We have something private to discuss.'

I left them and went back to my room, where I found Laura now sitting up on my bed, her back against the wall. She began to gnaw at a thumbnail – something that always made Pop angry. 'What were they saying?' she asked. I told her I didn't know but that Mother had asked me to leave the room and had said that it was something private. 'Oh lordy!' She now began to gnaw at the nail on her forefinger.

'What's this all about?'

She shook her head.

'Tell me.'

Finally I got it out of her. 'That man,' she said.

'What man?'

'That man in Holland Park.'

'Oh, that! But what has Mrs Bacon . . . ?'

'I told Angela about it.'

After Mrs Bacon had gone, we expected Mother to say something. But she went into the kitchen, where we heard her moving about as she fried some sausages and mixed some Smash for our supper. 'Children!' she eventually called. As we ate, she still said nothing, but she was unusually silent, putting now one elbow and now the other and sometimes both on the table, in the way that she was so often telling us not to sit at mealtimes. She looked thoughtful more than troubled.

A few days later Pop came home. He was even more tired and in an even worse temper than usual because he had had a puncture on the way. We tiptoed round the flat and then, even though the rain was coming down in buckets, we wandered out with

Benny. He had to be dragged along the High Street and kept trying to take shelter under the awnings of shops. When we returned home, just before lunchtime, we heard Pop shouting at Mother in the bedroom as we opened the door. 'Good God, woman, didn't you go to the police?'

We remained without moving in the small, square, high-ceilinged hall that was so dark, with its frosted window on to the well of the block, that it was as though we were standing in a cellar. We didn't hear Mother's answer.

Pop went on: 'And didn't you tell her never to go into that goddamn park again?'

This time we heard: 'No. After all, it's not likely to happen again.'

'It could easily happen again. What do you mean? That kind of pervert tends to hang around the same place, just like a dog going back to the same lamp-post.'

Mother said something inaudible and then, her voice louder now: 'One doesn't want to make too much of it.'

'Make too much of it! One can't make too much of it!' Laura had begun to gnaw at a thumbnail. I wanted to stop her. Pop would notice, as he always did, and that would make him even crosser. 'That kind of pervert is a menace to any child that goes into the goddamn park.'

'She'll forget about it. If it had made any real impression on her, I'd have known. By talking about it – by making a fuss about it. . . .'

'For Chrissake!' Pop bellowed that.

I shut the front door noisily behind us, at which Mother said, 'Sh! There they are – back from their walk!'

'Well, tell them to come and see me. Now. Here. Pronto!'

Pop still lay under the bedclothes, his chin blue because he hadn't shaved yet, his eyes bleary and one side of his face creased, as though with a scar, where he had been lying on it. 'Come here, Laura baby,' he said, patting the eiderdown beside him. 'Pop wants a word with his little girl.' I knew that Laura was frightened and that she did not want to go and sit that close to

Pop. But she walked over, slightly zigzag and knock-kneed in the way that always meant that she was shy or nervous, and sat upright beside him, her legs dangling over the side of the bed. He pulled her towards him, so that she now rested against his shoulder. 'Laura honey,' he said. 'Mother tells me something nasty happened to you in the park.' Laura did not answer. 'Laura?'

Mother, who was standing by the door, next to me, cut in: 'Oh, do leave it!' She was on the verge of crying, I could tell.

'Laura, are you listening to me? Is my little girl really and truly listening? Now, if anything like that happens again, ever, *ever*, I want to you look and see if you can find one of those keepers or a policeman. And, if you can't, well, honey, just tell one of the other people in the park – one of the grown-ups, I mean – and he or she will know exactly what to do. And if there's no one handy in the park, then just you come home, straight home as quick as you can run, and tell Mother all about it. Got it? Laura? Now, don't bite your nails, honey! You know how Pop hates you to spoil your lovely little hands. Laura!' He gave her a sharp little shake with the arm that was still around her and, like a doll's, her head flopped forward and then back again.

'Now, son.' I had been dreading this all the time that I had been standing by the door. He put up a hand and beckoned and step by step, I approached him, as though with that beckoning, finger he was pulling on a string attached to me.

'Yes, Pop.' I had to clear my throat before I spoke.

'Did you see this guy?'

'No, Pop.'

'How come?'

'What do you mean?'

'Well – just that. How come? Weren't you and Laura there together?'

'Yes, Pop. . . . But – well – we'd separated.'

'You mean you left your little sister while you wandered off some place?'

'No, Pop. I mean . . . I wanted to watch the tennis and she wanted to go to the playground to see if – if any of her friends were there.'

'I see. I get the picture.' He seemed about to say something else but instead stared at me so intensely, almost as though he were accusing me of something, that I felt the sweat breaking out all over my body. 'Now, look, son. So that you can go on going to that fine expensive school of yours and so that little Laura can go on going to hers, I've had to make big, big sacrifices. I've had to leave you all down here in London and I've had to go and live in unmarried quarters up there in Scotland without Mother to look after me. Now, haven't I? Well, when I'm away, I've got to be able to feel that I can rely on you to take my place. I mean, it's worrying enough as it is, me being so far away and not knowing from one moment to the next how you all are making out down here. I've got to be able to rely on you to look after your baby sister.' Again he stared at me and again I felt hot and sticky all over my body. Mother's arm was suddenly around my shoulders, but somehow I didn't want it there because – I don't know why – I felt that that might make things even worse for me with Pop. And I think that I was right, because he at once asked, not in the soft, sorrowful kind of voice that he had been using so far, but sharply, 'Didn't Laura tell you what had happened to her?'

'Yes, Pop.' Again I had to clear my throat before I could answer.

'And you didn't go and look for this man?'

'No, Pop.'

'You didn't feel you should go and look for him and ask him what the hell it was that he was doing to your little sister?'

'I suppose I thought . . . I thought it was too late by then to find him.'

'You *supposed*! Fine! . . . Look, son, you're almost a man now. A man would have gone and knocked a degenerate like that down.'

Mother was trying to draw me closer to her, but I resisted.

'You didn't even think of looking for one of those park attendants?' Silence. 'Or a policeman?' Silence. 'Hell, what kind of brother are you?'

Mother began, 'He probably never realized –' but Pop cut her short:

'You never even told your mother, your own mother!'

He threw his legs out of the bed, his arm still about Laura's waist. I saw that he was wearing nothing but his vest and underpants. Somehow, though I had often seen him like that before, I was now realizing for the first time how thin and hairy his legs were. 'Well, I guess it's about time for chow.' Suddenly he had become good-humoured and smiling. 'What have you got for us, Mother?'

Mother mumbled, 'Steak-and-kidney pie.'

'Steak-and-kidney pie as only Mother can make it!' Mother always bought frozen steak-and-kidney pie, but neither she nor Laura nor I ever let on. 'Now, Laura honey, Pop must get dressed.' Laura clambered off the bed, her lower lip trembling and her eyelashes blinking as though, as on that day when she saw the man, she did not know whether to laugh or cry. He got to his feet. 'Now, Laura, if anything like this happens again, you know what Pop wants you to do?'

'Yes, Pop.'

'And, son, you've got it straight now, haven't you?'

'Yes, Pop.'

'We've got to get the police to act on this pronto, if it ever happens again. Otherwise some other little girl is going to be exposed to the same kind of filth. Or worse. In fact, after lunch I'm going to put on my uniform and I'm going along to see the police to tell them. They ought to be warned. . . . OK. Now, run along, all of you. And make sure, Mother, that I have a big, big serving of that steak-and-kidney pie of yours. Don't let the kids eat all of it before I get to it!'

Laura usually walked home from school across Holland Park. If she didn't, it meant going all the way down Holland Walk, along Kensington High Street and then up Melbury Road. Angela – whose home, a big house, not a flat, was in the street next to ours – often walked with her. But she and Laura were always having silly little tiffs and then Laura would walk with someone else for a day or two. Because she was so pretty and so good at netball, and perhaps also because she spoke with that American accent, there was always a lot of competition for this honour.

About ten days after Pop had spoken to us about the man, I had just got back from St Paul's and was having a cup of tea with Mother in the kitchen, when Laura rushed in. (Each of us had a key to the front door, since Mother so often went out to visit the aunts.) At first, from her excited face, I thought that she must have some good news from school – there was to be an unexpected holiday, she had come top of her form, she had been invited to a party or away for the weekend. But instead she cried out, 'It's happened again! It's happened again! He did it again!'

Mother got to her feet, her cup still in her hand. She looked horribly upset, but I had the feeling – I don't know why – that she was even more upset by Laura's excitement than by its cause. 'Now take off your hat and put your satchel down. Then come and sit here and tell me.'

'But, Mother, he did it again! And Pop said – '

'Come and sit down, dear,' Mother repeated in a soft but firm voice. She pulled out a chair.

Laura sat on it, right on the edge. Her eyes were as bright as that time when she had had a high fever with measles.

'Were you alone?' Mother asked.

'Yes. Angela was going to walk with me but then Miss Barlow called her back about her music lesson and so I thought I wouldn't wait for her. And then – '

'Weren't there any other girls you could have walked with?'

'They'd all set off by then. I thought I might catch someone up.' She gnawed at a thumbnail. I could hear the click-click-click of her teeth on it. 'Oh, Mother, it was *horrible*!'

'Now, tell me – quietly and calmly – exactly what happened, dear.'

'Well, I was walking along, just beyond the Youth Hostel. I was walking quite fast. And then – then – well, there he was!'

'Where, dear?'

'In the bushes. And he opened his raincoat, this long grey raincoat, and then . . .' Suddenly she began to sob, her arms crossed on the kitchen table and her cheek resting on them.

Mother sighed, looked at me and then got up. Her face was sad and somehow distant, as though she were thinking not of what had just happened but of something long ago. 'Darling. Darling. Now, come along.' She was stooping over Laura. 'It's not all that bad or all that important.' Laura continued to sob loudly. 'Are you sure it was the same man?'

Laura jerked up. 'Don't you believe me?' she wailed.

'Of course I believe you, darling, but are you sure . . .?'

'Of course I'm sure! He – he was wearing this same grey raincoat; it's a long raincoat, grey, oh, almost to his ankles – no, not almost to his ankles but, oh, far below his knees. And glasses – the sun was on them so I couldn't see his eyes, though I knew that he was staring at me. And this funny cap, a cap with a peak, like – like a schoolboy's almost – like that one that Angela's brother wears. Of *course* it was the same man! Oh, Mother, it was *horrible*! Beastly! I wish Pop was here!'

The mention of Pop seemed to make Mother stiffen and straighten in her chair, as though she had remembered something suddenly. 'Give her some tea or orange juice,' she said to me. 'Look after her. I'm just going to the telephone.'

'Who are you going to telephone?' Laura asked. But Mother left the room without giving any answer.

'Do you want some tea?' I asked. I felt embarrassed and not at all sure how to cope with Laura by herself. It was as though she had suddenly become a stranger.

She shook her head and then put out a hand and began to stir the sugar, slowly round and round, in the bowl. 'You believe me, don't you?'

I nodded. 'Why not? Why should you lie about it or make it up?' I could hear Mother talking on the telephone in the next room but I couldn't hear what she was saying.

'You probably think this is all a lot of fuss about nothing.'

It was, in fact, what I did think, but I shook my head.

'It's difficult for a boy to understand.'

Mother came back. 'The police'll be here as soon as possible.'

'The police!' Laura was terrified. 'Oh, Mother!'

'Pop said that I must ring them. Don't you remember? They sounded very nice and understanding.'

'Oh, but I wish . . .'

'I had to do what Pop told us to do.'

In no time at all there was a ring at the bell and there were these two policemen, one old and slightly shrivelled and grey-looking with a West Country accent, and the other square-shouldered and young, with long reddish hair that reached over his collar and a straggling reddish moustache that all but covered his small irregular teeth. I must say they were very polite and sympathetic, talking in the kind of quiet voices that people use when you are ill and addressing Mother as 'mam' and Laura as 'miss'. After they had been told how everything had happened, the older one asked Laura and Mother to go with them in the car to see if they could spot the man in the park.

'Oh but he's sure to have gone by now,' Mother said as though she were not at all eager to go with them.

'You never know, mam,' the older policeman said. 'You just can't say in these cases. Sometimes they hang about waiting for another victim. You can't expect them to behave as an ordinary person would.'

'It's worth a try,' said the other one.

'There's nothing to be afraid of, miss. We'll be there to protect you. All we want is for you to point him out if you spot him.'

The four of them eventually left and I tried to settle to my homework. But I felt restless and somehow uneasy, and so eventually I took one of the cigarettes from the box in the sitting-room and smoked that while looking out of the window for their return. I opened the window wide and hoped that Mother wouldn't smell anything.

After about half an hour the car drew up at the kerb and Mother and Laura got out. Mother said something I couldn't hear to the men inside the car, and then I heard the young one's voice as he leaned out of the window, booming at her so that any neighbour who was around could have heard: 'Well, don't hesitate to call us if it ever happens again. That's what we're here for.' I knew then that they hadn't been able to find the man and I threw what was left of the cigarette out of the window and hurried back to my homework.

'Well?' I asked, looking up as they came in.

'No sign of him,' Mother sighed.

'I knew he wouldn't be there any longer,' Laura said. 'It was just a waste of time.'

'Well, there was nothing else they could do. They did their best. They were really very helpful and nice.'

'I *hated* the younger one!'

'Don't be silly! Why should you hate him?'

'I think he thought I'd imagined it all.'

'I don't think he thought anything of the kind.' Mother looked tired and pale. She went and flopped down in one of the two armchairs, the one that Pop usually used, and stared into the empty grate with its fan of greying paper. 'I've been thinking,' she said. 'Perhaps it would be better not to tell Pop all about this. It'll only upset him. You know how tired he always is on his visits.' She did not look at either of us, and neither of us said anything. 'Children?'

'As you like, Mother,' I replied.

Laura said nothing.

I think that I knew even then that Laura would not do as Mother asked. I'm not sure exactly how she came to tell Pop – whether he asked her or whether she volunteered – but she had been in his room, after he had woken from his sleep but was still lying in bed, and then, all at once, there he was, his hair standing on end and his face all red and crumpled, shouting in nothing but his vest and underpants and a pair of socks that were hanging round his ankles. 'Mother! Mother! Come here, will you!'

Mother came out of the kitchen, where she had been at work on the lunch, and I put my head round the door to see what the row was all about. Pop squinted at me in a puzzled, vaguely hostile way. 'Did I call for you, son?' he demanded.

'No, Pop.'

'Well, then, beat it!'

I disappeared behind the door and gave it a little push, so as not to shut it completely.

I heard: 'Laura's just been telling me that that goddamn bastard has been up to his tricks again.'

I could hear no answer from Mother; perhaps she merely nodded.

'Well, for Christ's sake, why didn't you tell me? Don't I have a right to know? I've telephoned here, oh, at least half a dozen times and you've said not a word.'

'I didn't want to upset you – worry you. You've so much else on your mind.'

'I haven't so much on my mind that I don't need to worry about my little girl having another experience of that kind. Are you crazy?'

'I called the police at once. Just as you told me.'

'And a hell of a lot of good they seem to have been!'

'They did their best. They came here in a car and then they – '

'Yeah, yeah! I've heard it all from Laura. It turns me up, the whole thing turns me up. Christ, what's happening to this country?'

He went on for a long, long time like that, until Mother said, quietly but firmly, that she must get back to the kitchen or else the lunch would get spoiled.

Pop ate a huge lunch and, as so often after he has made one of his scenes, he was in the best of moods. He even poured me out some beer when he poured out some for himself and he kept us all laughing with some long story about 'two long-haired

E

hippies' who had thumbed a hitch-hike from him. Lunch over, he belched loudly, making Laura and me laugh even more than at the end of the story, and then he smacked a knee with either palm and said, 'Well, kids, how about it? I want to see this Bicentennial Exhibition at Greenwich. Are you both game?'

Neither of us was too keen to see the Exhibition, but Laura screeched, 'Oh, Pop! How terrific!' and I said, 'Fine!'

It was a sunny day, but a cold wind was blowing; and Pop, who always felt the cold more than any of us – he was always saying 'this weather in Britain gets into my bones' – told us that we should go downstairs into the saloon of the boat to Greenwich. 'Oh, but, Pop, we won't be able to see anything from there!' Laura protested, but he said that he didn't want his little girl running around with a runny nose or in bed with a chill and she was to be a good girl and do what he told her. 'Now, would you believe that! Christ!' he exclaimed, looking around the saloon, which was empty but for a single elderly couple who were sitting up very stiff and straight with quite a distance between them. 'Well!' He meant that the bar had an iron grille across it and there was not a chance of a drink. He got a hip flask out of his trousers and took a swig from that. Bourbon. That was always his drink in England as it is now in the States. He wiped his mouth on the back of his hand, apparently unaware that the elderly couple had been staring at him in disapproval, and then sat down on the cracked leather seat that ran along the wall on the other side. 'Well, is my best girl going to sit beside me?' Laura sat down next to him; but she was soon up again, kneeling on the seat in order to look out of the porthole. I remained standing. It was stuffy down there and everything smelled of diesel oil and stale cigarette smoke. I began to feel slightly sick.

When we had been travelling for about five minutes, Laura said, 'Pop, mayn't I just go up on deck for the teeniest weeniest while? I can't see *at all* from here.' She had been sitting down and then jumping up again and rushing from porthole to port-hole.

'OK, honey. But make it short and sweet. And this brother of yours had better tag along to keep an eye on you. Don't lean over the rail and don't talk to any of those foreign students I saw up there, even if they talk to you.'

'Thanks, Pop. 'Bye!'

She ran up the companionway, and I followed after her. Pop shouted something about not taking her cardigan off, but either she did not hear him or she pretended not to hear.

It was such fun up on deck, trying to recognize one landmark after another – the Houses of Parliament, the dome of St Paul's, the Monument, Wapping Old Stairs – and watching the little motorboats and the barges and the sailing dinghies, that we both forgot all about Pop. We even forgot what he had told us about not talking to the students. One of them, a skinny boy of about my age, in shorts and a tee-shirt – his knobbly knees and elbows and knuckles were blue with cold – pointed to the Hayward Gallery and said, in a French accent, 'Excuse me – prison?' and then we corrected him and we all began laughing and so we got into conversation with the whole lot of them.

Suddenly Pop was there, the wind blowing his trousers tight against his legs and his hair over to one side so that one could see the bald patch that he usually kept hidden. 'Laura!' he bawled. At that moment he seemed to be angrier with her than with me. 'Now, what did I tell you? This is a nice way to behave when I take you on a treat!' He looked at her. '*And* you've undone that cardigan.'

'Oh, Pop, I'm sorry, but it was so lovely up here and really not at all cold, not at all cold, Pop.'

'Well, what do you think it was like for me down below – all on my own while you two were fooling around up here together? You'd forgotten all about your Pop – now, hadn't you? He might have been miles and miles away in Scotland for all you cared.'

'Oh, Pop!' She ran to him and took his hand, pressing her cheek against his windcheater, and I could see that, though he was now squinting at me in that way of his when I had made him angry, he was going to forgive us. 'OK, OK!' he said. 'But Pop has certainly got himself a very, very disobedient little sweetheart.' He ran a hand through her hair, and at the same moment the boat let out a long wail. We were about to dock.

The next time that Laura said that she had seen the man, she had been with Angela. The two girls ran back to the school – because it was nearer than their homes, they said – and told the head-mistress what had happened. She at once telephoned to the police and again a police car hurried over. The crew were different from the other time – 'much nicer', Laura said. The two men and the two girls drove round and round the park, even going up and down paths meant only for pedestrians, but the man had vanished as before.

Mrs Bacon again visited Mother, bringing Angela with her but sending her into Laura's room while the two mothers talked. From my room it was impossible to hear what they were saying to each other; but at the door, as she was leaving – I was in the hall, too – she turned to Mother. 'Well, if you don't feel inclined to come and see Miss Pratt with me, at least I can tell her that you agree with me one hundred per cent, can't I?'

'What are you going to see Miss Pratt about?' Angela asked, looking across at Laura and then, when she caught her eye, putting a hand up to cup her mouth as though she were going either to giggle or cough.

'Never mind, dear.' Mrs Bacon turned once more to Mother. 'I can say that we're completely at one over this?'

Mother looked doubtful, as she said in a flat tired voice, 'Oh, yes, I think so.'

'Good,' Mrs Bacon said firmly. 'Then, I'll see her first thing tomorrow.'

Later I learned that Mrs Bacon had asked the headmistress to tell all the girls not to go into the park, but that Miss Pratt had thought this 'altogether too drastic' since there had been only two reported incidents of that kind to date. Mrs Bacon told Mother this in the forecourt outside Barkers, where we had run into her while the two of us were doing the weekend shopping. I was carrying Mother's basket, making Mrs Bacon comment: 'How nice to have a stalwart young man to do one's carrying for one!' She was wearing another coal-scuttle hat, this time bright blue, not red, with a spray of feathers, dyed a darker blue, pinned to one side. 'That woman is quite incapable of any kind of decisive action. She just dithers.' She was talking about Miss Pratt, but it seemed to me almost as if she were talking about Mother, and Mother seemed to feel that, too, as she began to blush and look uneasy. 'It was the same when those boys from the comprehensive used to shout things over the wall. Hopeless. Well, at all events, I've told my Angela that from now on she's not to set foot in the park. That's flat.'

'It's an awful long way round to the school for them,' Mother said. 'And worse back after a tiring day.'

'Well, better an extra quarter of an hour than a repetition,' Mrs Bacon said firmly, shifting her basket from one hand to the other. She leaned forward to Mother and lowered her voice as though she thought that that was enough to prevent my hearing: 'I do think that exhibitionism is such an extraordinary thing. I always have. It's the only sexual – er – peculiarity that is turned entirely against its object. Isn't it? There's no desire to attract, the purpose is not to achieve any kind of – er – communication. Just the opposite. What it does is disgust and repel.'

Mother nodded, gave me a nervous glance and nodded again.

As we left Mrs Bacon, Mother sighed: 'Oh dear.' She made no other comment.

When Pop came home the following weekend and learned that the man had shown himself to Laura yet again, he became even more frantic than on the other occasions. Instead of going to bed after breakfast, he stormed at Mother for most of the morning. Why hadn't she spoken to the police herself? Why hadn't she gone with Mrs Bacon to see Miss Pratt? Why hadn't she forbidden Laura to go into the park again? He kept pouring out beer for himself – he had taken off his jacket and shirt and in spite of that he was sweating freely – and, as he gulped it down, glass after glass, he kept thinking of something fresh to say. I felt sorry for him – almost as sorry for him as for Mother. He kept repeating how terrible it was for him to be so far away, up there in that goddamn place way out in the sticks, not knowing what was happening to his loved ones, not able to protect them, not able to guide them. Eventually Mother began to cry and then, between sobs, she told me to go to my room and Laura to go to hers. Or else, she said, we could have a walk before lunch. 'But not in that park, for Christ's sake, not in that park!' Pop took his head out of his hands to shout. 'Because that boy is certainly not going to be able to cope with the situation if that maniac appears.' Laura had all this time been playing patience in a corner on the floor. She had not seemed to be interested at all in what was going on, and when we were out in the street and I said, 'What a lot of fuss! It's given me quite a headache,' she only said, ignoring my remark, 'There's no reason why we shouldn't go to Kensington Gardens. We can watch all those silly old men flying kites.'

That night, after we had been sent to bed at nine, I could hear Pop going on and on at Mother in the next room even though I could seldom hear what she was saying. 'I know about these things. . . . Well, for Pete's sake, I did a course in psychiatry in college – which is more than you ever did. . . . A shock like that can turn off a young girl for life. . . . Well, of course it can! . . . Of *course*! . . . Everyone knows that. . . . It can make her goddamn frigid for life. . . . Half these frigid women have had some kind of shock like that way back in their childhoods. It's been proved. . . . And I want my little Laura to grow up into a thoroughly normal healthy woman. . . . Is that too much for a father to want for his daughter? . . . Well, is it? Is it?'

I pulled the bedclothes over my head and decided to go to sleep.

Laura now had to walk the long way to and from school, and that meant that she had to set off earlier and came back later. I guessed that on some days, especially when it was raining or when she didn't want to miss some programme on the telly, she disobeyed Pop's orders and cut across the park. I suspect that Angela also sometimes disobeyed Mrs Bacon. Certainly, one afternoon when I was taking the dog for a walk after I had come home from school, I saw the two girls coming out of the lower gate. They looked surprised and disconcerted and for a moment I even thought that they were going to pretend that they hadn't noticed me so near to them. 'I thought that you'd been strictly forbidden to go into the park,' I said, not seriously but to tease them.

'We just slipped in to see about that pop concert in the open-air theatre on Sunday afternoon,' Angela put in quickly. 'That was all. Only for a moment. You won't tell on us, will you?'

'Of course not.'

'There was no sign of *him*,' Laura said.

'Thank goodness,' Angela added. Then they both began to giggle.

'D'you want to come back in with me and the dog?'

'Oh, no! We'd better not,' Angela said.

'We daren't!' Laura added. 'Pop told me that, even with you, I was never to go in. And Mr and Mrs Bacon both told Angela that on no account – '

'Please yourselves!' I said. I was quite glad not to have them with me, whispering and giggling together and making remarks to each other that I usually did not understand and did not wish to understand.

It was two or three days after that that Laura came back from school accompanied by a thin, spectacled, middle-aged woman in a shabby coat with one button hanging loose on its front. 'I've brought your little girl back home,' she said when Mother answered the ring at the door. 'She seems to have had a rather nasty little experience.' Laura stood behind her, as though for protection. I wondered why she hadn't opened the door with her key. 'I expect she'll tell you all about it herself,' the woman went on.

'Oh, not again!' Mother gasped.

'Has it happened before? Oh, my word!'

Laura looked quite calm as she now came out from behind the woman, put down her satchel and began to take off her hat and blazer.

Mother nodded. 'Yes, I'm afraid so. More than once.'

'I looked to see if the dirty brute was still there – she said he was in one of those telephone kiosks just at the end of Kensington Walk – but of course he'd beat it. Just as well! If I'd got my hands on him – '

'I'm awfully grateful to you,' Mother said.

'The little girl wanted to call the police,' the woman went on, first fiddling with the dangling button and then giving it a sharp tug so that it came away in her hand. 'But, since he was no longer there, there didn't seem any point. Besides – to be absolutely truthful with you – I'm hurrying home to get my old man his tea and I'll be late as it is.'

'Oh, I *am* sorry!' Mother said. 'Oh dear!'

'Not to worry. He'll have to wait for a change. I'll hop on the twenty-eight outside the Odeon.'

By now Laura had gone into the kitchen and had started to pour out for herself some orange juice from the jug in the fridge. Mother followed her there and I came in behind her. She watched Laura for a time as though uncertain how to begin. Then she said, 'Laura dear.'

'Yes, Mother.' Laura sipped daintily. The sunshine through the window glinted on her fair hair and on one of her cheekbones, and I thought: Yes, Pop *is* right when he's always telling her how pretty she is.

'Laura. I want you to be absolutely truthful with me.'

'Yes, Mother.' She sipped again.

'Did you really see that man or did you . . . ?' She faltered there.

'Yes, Mother?'

'Or did you just imagine it?'

'Imagine, Mother? Why should I imagine it? *Of course* I saw him. It was broad daylight, you know that, and there he was in the kiosk and, as I passed, he opened the door and then he opened that horrible long grey raincoat – by then he was holding the door open with a foot – and – and – '

'All right, dear.'

'Don't you *believe* me, Mother?' Suddenly she banged the glass of half-finished orange juice down on the table, so hard that I thought she would break it, and no less suddenly there were tears in her eyes.

'Of course, darling!' Mother put an arm round her. 'It was a beastly experience. Now, I want you to forget all about it.'

'But I can't, I can't!' Laura wailed.

'Now, Laura . . . Please . . . Don't be silly. . . .'

Laura was sobbing helplessly, and no less helplessly Mother looked across at me. But I had no idea what to do about it. I knew that Pop would get even more frantic when he heard of this latest appearance of the man, and of course I was right.

Pop was having ten days' leave when the man showed himself to Laura for the last time. It had been raining all afternoon, a steady downpour, and for the first time one realized that another summer was over. Mother had come into the sitting-room, where I was busy with my homework and Pop was reading a detective novel, and had hugged herself in the way that she does when she is cold and had asked whether we didn't want the fire on. But Pop said no, she knew that we had to economize, if she was that cold why didn't she put on a sweater or cardigan? Mother replied in a soft distant voice, 'I was thinking of you. You always feel the cold more than the rest of us,' and Pop then said, 'Well, thanks, honey,' in a tone that might or might not have been sarcastic.

A little later Pop stirred in the armchair, took out a handkerchief and blew his nose loudly – he had been complaining again of his catarrh – and then looked at his watch and asked, 'What's happened to that little girl of mine?'

I did not answer, since he seemed to be putting the question to himself and not to me, and then he said, '*You* don't care, do you?'

I looked up from my work, surprised, and said, 'Don't care what?'

'*You* don't care a fuck what's happened to her!' I did not answer. 'No, of course you don't. Boy, what a brother!'

It was only a few seconds after that that there was a ring at the bell, followed at once by the sound of a key in the lock of the front door. 'What the hell – ?' Pop jumped to his feet, the detective story in one hand, and at the same moment Laura ran in. 'He did it again, he did it again!' she screamed, running up to Pop and throwing her arms around him. 'Oh, Pop! He was there!'

'Where?' Pop asked. 'Where, Laura? Where?'

Mother came in at all this commotion, looked at them both and said, 'Laura! You haven't been in that park!'

Laura began to sob, still clutching at Pop. 'I had to go that way. It's pouring outside and I hadn't got a mac or an umbrella or anything. I'm soaked. Look at me!'

'I told you to take your mac this morning at breakfast,' Mother said.

'What the hell is the use of telling the kid that now?' Pop shouted at her. 'Here, Laura, wait a sec. We're going to find him. This time we're going to get him! These goddamn British cops are no fucking use. We'll get him together, sweetie.' He ran out of the room, into the bedroom that he and Mother shared, and Mother followed him. I heard her cry out, 'What are you doing? What d'you want that thing for? Pop!' But he just shouted at her, 'Oh, get lost!'

He was putting something into the pocket of his service raincoat as he came out. 'Come on, Laura! Come on, sweetie! Come with Pop!'

'You're not taking her with you?' Mother said,

'Certainly I'm taking her with me. How the fucking else am I to recognize the bastard?'

'But she's all wet,' Mother said.

Pop paid no attention to that. He looked at me. 'And you, too.'

'Me?'

'Yeah, you. Not that you're likely to be of much help to me, Sir Laurence. *Move!* Come on, *move!*'

I got up and went into the hall.

'Take your mac,' Mother said. 'And you, too, Laura.' I took mine down from the peg, but Laura did not seem to have heard. Mother went on: 'Look, you don't need to drag the children into all this – '

But Pop wasn't listening. 'Come on, honey!' He put an arm round Laura's shoulders and pushed her out of the front door. Then he made a gesture with his head at me. 'O K. Out. Pronto.'

He told me to get into the back of the car and Laura to get in front beside him. There was a lot of cursing under his breath as the engine died on him two or three times. 'Too much choke, too much fucking choke,' he muttered. Then, at last, we were moving. 'Now, honey, you tell Pop exactly where he was. Because Pop is going to find that bastard, come what may.'

Laura didn't seem to be in the least bit frightened now. I was amazed by her calmness as she directed him: 'This way, Pop,' or 'Turn right, Pop.' Finally she said, 'He was up there, Pop. But cars can't go there.'

'Like hell they can't!' Pop muttered between his teeth, and the car began lurching up the narrow path between dripping bushes. Because of the heavy rain, we saw no one but a man with an umbrella, with a little dog, all huddled up, trailing behind him on a lead. 'Is that him?' Pop demanded, and Laura replied, with a little giggle, 'No, Pop. He doesn't look at all like that. Like I said, he has this long grey raincoat and this funny cap.'

I don't think I really believed that the man had been in the park that afternoon with all that rain – I was sure that Laura had imagined it all or had made it up as some weird kind of joke –

when suddenly there he was, about two hundred yards ahead of us, walking quickly up the path, his hands deep in the pockets of the raincoat and his shoulders hunched, just as she had described him.

'That's him, Pop!' Laura cried out excitedly. 'That's him! There in front of us!'

'Are you sure?'

'Of course I'm sure! It's the raincoat and the cap and the way he . . . Oh, Pop!'

As though, without looking round, the man knew that we were driving up closer and closer behind him and were not on the road on the other side of the fence, he all at once left this path for another, narrower one that wound into the woods. It was impossible to follow him any longer in the car. Pop braked sharply. 'Now, Laura,' he said, 'I want you to be a good girl and do what Pop tells you. As soon as we leave this car, I want you to lock it all round. Got that? *Lock it all round!* 'Cos I don't want anything nasty to happen to my little girl.' He looked over his shoulder at me. 'O K. Out!' I hesitated. '*Out!*'

We plunged down the path, Pop lurching from time to time so that the bushes made a swishing sound against his army raincoat. He was gaining on the man and leaving me behind him. Then the man began to run and Pop began to run, too. I trotted behind them. I didn't really want to be there when Pop caught him up.

Pop is no athlete – even then he had this small pot in front, I suppose from all that beer-drinking – but the man was really feeble. He darted from one side to another, just as I saw a mouse doing when Benny cornered it in the hall, and I could hear him cry out in his high-pitched educated voice, 'What do you want? Who are you? What is it? Please!'

Pop had grabbed him. 'This is a citizen's arrest,' he said. 'So you'd better come quietly. Or else.'

The man wriggled in his grip. 'I don't understand. What do you mean? What is this all about?' Now he was whimpering. He wore thick glasses with heavy steel frames and they were all dotted with raindrops. I wondered how much he could see of us.

'You've been molesting my little girl,' Pop said. 'That's what you've been doing. She's back there in that locked car over there and she's picked you out for me. There's no doubt about it. No doubt at all!'

In a husky voice, no longer whimpering, the man said, 'All right. All right. I'll come. But just let go of me. You're hurting my arm. I don't know what. I don't know why.' He pushed the glasses up his nose with one hand and I saw that the sleeve of the raincoat was too long, covering the hand almost to the fingertips. 'All right.' He was still out of breath and so was Pop. Both their faces looked yellow in the gloom under the dripping trees, and the cap was all sodden, so that it looked as though it had a stain in the middle of it. Pop's hair lay in wet prongs on his forehead.

'OK,' Pop said to me. 'Get the other side of him. We don't want any funny stuff.' I stood on one side of the man and Pop was on the other. Suddenly Pop had become strangely calm, almost as though he were stupefied. 'I have to do this,' he said. 'You see that, don't you?' He might have been apologizing.

The man's reply surprised me. In that high-pitched educated voice he said, 'And I have to do it, too. Can't help myself.' We had begun to walk. 'It's terrible. Terrible really. I've been in trouble before. Not here, in Eastbourne. And before that, oh, years ago, I was only a student, in a cinema at Oxford. I'm a married man. Three kids. I don't know why. I don't know how. A compulsion. Can't get away from it.' He was still breathless and the words came out in spurts.

Pop sounded sympathetic as he answered, 'Yeah. OK. But you can't do that kind of thing to a little girl. Not to a little girl like my Laura. How can you dirty up a young life as fine and pure as that? Christ! I mean, I see you've got your problem, but Christ – !'

Suddenly the man halted and put his hands to his stomach, hunching himself over as he did so. 'Oh God!' he said. 'Oh!' His face looked even yellower.

'What's the matter?' Pop asked, still in that strangely sympathetic tone.

'I think. I think that. I think that I'm. Going to be sick.' His face was screwed up now and the words again came out in spurts.

'Well, don't throw up on us!' Pop shouted, and suddenly all the sympathy had disappeared and he sounded angry and vindictive once again. 'Go and throw up over there!'

The man started gagging. Then he took a few steps away from us and started gagging again. Then he took a few more steps and some saliva glistened as it shot from his mouth and dribbled down his chin. Long before Pop I knew what he was planning and I was ready for him. All at once he raced for the tree by the wall.

I was amazed that that middle-aged, narrow-shouldered, breathless man should suddenly show so much speed and agility. He jumped into the fork of the tree and then a hand went out, half-concealed by the sleeve of the long grey raincoat, and reached for the top of the wall. 'Get him!' Pop shouted. 'Go on! Get him!' But I had already got him by one leg and was pulling at him. Then I heard Pop shout, 'Don't move! Don't move! If you move, you've had it!' I turned my head, still holding the man's leg with one hand and a tail of his raincoat with the other. Then I saw what Pop was holding in his hand. 'It's all right!' I shouted. 'Pop!' Pop was squinting at me (however I try to remember if differently, he is always squinting at me and not at the man) in the way that he does even now when he's angry with me. 'Pop!' I shouted again. He was still squinting at me. Then the gun exploded. I let go of the man and began to run away. I remember thinking as I ran: Am I alive? Am I still alive? Has he wounded me? Then I heard another shot. I looked over my shoulder and the man was tumbling down off the tree, his raincoat catching on a little branch below the fork and tearing as he fell. Pop began to walk over to him slowly. Then be turned and yelled at me: 'Come back, you little coward! Come hack here!'

The man now looked like one of those mysterious bundles of ragged and sodden clothes that you sometimes find lying under bushes in parks. Pop turned him over with his foot and stared down. I came closer, my mouth tasting horribly of the explosions from the gun – or perhaps I only smelled them. The rain was spattering on the upturned glasses and on the sticking-out yellow nose, which now looked like the beak of a dead bird. I thought that he had already gone, but he opened his eyes and looked up at me and not at Pop, and then with a kind of surprise and hurt in his voice he said, 'That was. A very. A very uncivil thing to do.'

He had told us before that he wanted to be sick and, as his body strained and his lips came forward and his face screwed up again, I thought: He's going to do it now, he's going to be sick, as he said. But it was blood that at last flooded out.

Pop turned on me in a terrible fury. 'If you hadn't let him go like that – if you hadn't chickened out – !'

I had chickened out. That was how Pop told the story and that was how I also told it. Everyone was sympathetic both to me and to Pop. The judge, summing up, spoke of 'terrible provocation to a man living under the strain of a protracted separation from those dearest to him', of 'the foolhardiness of the wretched victim's attempt to escape retribution', of a 'young boy's perfectly natural but regrettable impulse to run away at a moment of crisis' and of Pop's 'blameless past'.

At the end of it all, Pop received a sentence of one year, suspended.

Was it like that? Sometimes I can almost persuade myself it was. But then, suddenly, I still see Pop squinting at me, always at me and not at the man, as he raises that revolver under the dripping trees in the gloom of the city woodland.

Little Old Lady Passing By

THE English rot that caused the wood of the windowsill to flake away in powdery fragments under the nail of Roz's forefinger was not the same as that Caribbean rot of growths strangled by stronger growths, of wood eroded by rain and myriads of parasites, and of flesh swelling and then assuming the shiny, rainbow hues of deliquescence. There was that rat, she could never forget that rat: Pa put down poison and then, days later, she had found it behind the kerosene cooker, its teeth a heap of ivory toothpicks and its skin a twitching tent for a host of pullulating maggots.

By the English sink, Roz continued to pick away at the English rot, while awaiting that moment when she must put on her coat, hat and gloves, and then descend all those steps (the lift again out of order) and stride out to the nursery school where little Kevin, his hair no longer flat as she had brushed it so carefully that morning and his clothes no longer clean and uncrumpled, would be standing by the wire netting, peering through it with dark, hungry eyes, until she called out his name. Other children waited on the concrete outside; but he would never do so, as though afraid that if he did not hook his fingers through that netting and keep it between himself and the world, then some imperious stranger might lay claim to him. But who? His father had long since vanished, with the white girl whom Roz had invited back to the council flat out of pity for her abject home-lessness on her discharge from hospital (the scars on her wrists were still ribbed and red and her shoulders still bowed, as though she were cringing from the next thump that she expected some brute of a man to give her) and it was unlikely that he would ever return to reclaim something that he had so obviously not wanted. One friend had said that he was back in gaol; another, that he had returned to Kingstown. The girl, both friends were sure, was dead. But the thought of her death gave Roz not the expected satisfaction, but a listless sadness. Like that rat, the poor creature had had strangely pointed, ivory-yellow teeth; and like the rat's belly, hers too had been swollen with a parasitic life not her own. This was the child, his child, that the friends had told Roz that she had 'lost', as she eventually lost all her possessions: battered suitcases and paper bags abandoned in left-luggage lockers and never reclaimed; coats hung up in pubs and forgotten; bracelets and bangles – how they would jangle, and how Roz's nerves would jangle with them, as the girl waddled about the flat – mysteriously falling off and never retrieved.

Roz looked out over the balcony outside the kitchen but she could not look down, to where children older than little Kevin had snapped off the saplings planted by a stout Lady Mayoress only a few weeks ago, daubed the walls of the garages, and reduced the grass to a bog. It was just as well that she could not look down, because it was so much pleasanter to look out at the sky, as it sharpened from glow to bright or blurred from bright to glimmer. Roz liked it when the large flakes of snow dithered down, like feathers from a burst eiderdown, past the rusty railings; when the starlings or the dead leaves whirled and wheeled in the same kind of ever-narrowing concentric circles; when an aeroplane (she would tilt her head on its firm, column-like neck) would leave a furry trail on an expanse of arctic blue. Every other tenant as high as this was always complaining; but she liked to be above it all, having so often wished in the past that that wood-and-corrugated iron shed of her childhood and adolescence were far, far above the smoky, evil-smelling pond out of which it emerged shakily on stilts.

Suddenly the old woman passed before her along the balcony outside the window, huddled, like some ancient peasant, under the shawl that covered her head and stooping shoulders and then fell to her waist. The shawl was brown and the old woman's face, on the rare occasions when Roz had been able to glimpse it, was also brown, with smooth prominent cheekbones and curious tucks on either side of a caved-in mouth, at either side of the rheumy eyes and between the evanescent eyebrows, as though the skin in those places had been drawn together with a surgical needle. She did not look round at Roz now – she never did so – while she made her way, shuffling and crablike, along the balcony with her head and body turned away from the railing, the ever-changing sky above it and the never-changing mess below it, as though she were frightened that, tiny as she was, she might suddenly be sucked up by some gust of wind, as those leaves and starlings were sucked up, and first be lifted high, high, and then be dashed to the earth. She was going to the dustbins, which were stacked on a service lift, as she went every day at precisely this hour; and, as always, she was carrying a brown-paper bag with her rubbish in it. She was plainly too old and too frail to carry a bin, however small, and it was invariably into Roz's bin, with 'No. 89' daubed on it, that she chose to empty the bag, shaking out its contents and then taking it back into her flat with her, refolded and tucked under an elbow, as though it were something precious. Roz had once or twice tried to address her but, having received no answer, not even a glimmer of acknowledgement, she had long since given up. She was called Mrs Simmons, that was all Roz knew about her; and from time to time – at the most, once a week – a tall, stooping man, greying hair brushed forward in a whorl and teeth too regular and gleaming to be genuine, would call to see her for an hour or two, sometimes accompanied by another, thick-set, younger man, who had a habit of hopping about on his toes while they waited for the door to open, as though, with his broken nose and puffy eyes, he were a boxer limbering up before a contest.

Roz now watched Mrs Simmons because there were still ten minutes to go before, the flat cleaned, the clothes washed and the vegetables prepared and soaking in water, she ran down all those steps with a clatter of heels on concrete. Mrs Simmons removed the lid of the dustbin; but then, instead of at once shaking out the contents of her bag, she peered down. A hand descended and she took out something. At first Roz thought angrily that it must be that letter that she had received that morning from Mom and that she had failed to tear up properly ('I jest hate to arsk you agen but its his playing the hosses . . .') But then she saw that what Mrs Simmons had removed was that Sunday supplement, weeks old, that she had asked one of the patients if she could take away with her, since it contained a recipe for making doughnuts and Kevin loved those. (In the event, the recipe had proved too troublesome – there was no yeast to be had in the cramped estate store, staffed by a Ugandan Indian and his clan of relatives of every age – and she had never got round to making them.) Mrs Simmons was now turning the pages, sodden with gravy and flecked with tealeaves that, from here, looked like clusters of flies. Then she slipped the supplement under her shawl and shuffled back along the balcony.

Roz was a kindly woman, forever performing for others services that were at worst resented and at best unreciprocated; and so she now opened the window and called out: 'I have a lot of those magazines. The patients give them to me. If you'd like . . .'

The old woman turned slowly; no less slowly straightened herself, so that the shawl slipped off her head to reveal scant tufts of grey hair cropped as close as a boy's; and then stared at Roz with eyes extraordinarily blue and penetrating between those curious tucks in the brown flesh on either side of them. Finally, in a hoarse, guttural voice, foreign in its accent, she replied curtly: 'Thank you. But it was just this magazine I wished to see. It has . . . something in it.'

Roz remained at the window long after the old woman had slipped back, like some nocturnal creature, from the brilliant light out on the balcony into the perpetually curtained gloom of her lair. What could that 'something' be? The recipe for dough-nuts? Her horoscope? That advertisement for a set of non-stick pans? (Roz herself had all but filled in the coupon and sent a cheque.) That article about Elton John? (Kevin would sit swinging his legs back and forth and laughing, laughing joyously, if ever one of his records was played on the transistor radio that stood on the table beside the humped bed in which mother and son would sleep in a tangle of shared bedclothes, odours and dreams.) Well, that's that, Roz thought. She doesn't want to be friendly. It's probably my colour. Except in the hospital, where they relied on her for pills, bedpans and late-night drinks, people seldom did want to be friendly. She was used to that, and this habitual friendlessness, so much more acute now that Reg no longer drifted home with his loud, lounging pals, was a strange source of pride to her. Oh, I'm better on my own, she had retorted when that nervous social worker had tried to sympathize with her. And I'm not really on my own, not ever. There's always Kevin, you see.

Yes, there was always Kevin, whom she was determined to bring up 'nice' and whose shoes were therefore always clean, his hair neatly plastered down with water, and his clothes scrupulously washed, ironed and mended. She did not like him to play with other children, white or black, on the estate, preferring to keep him always by her. She would trail him round the Commonwealth Institute or the Victoria and Albert Museum; she would make him watch programmes about wildlife and exploration on the television; she would turn on 'Your Hundred Best Tunes' on the transistor on Sunday evenings and coax him into listening, fidgety and intermittently bored, to that. When she was on duty at hours when he was not at school, she would leave him, not with one of the neighbours, but with Mrs Crombie, a professional childminder, who had been a nanny until her 'family', no longer able to put up with the tedium of her chatter or the cantankerousness of her ways now that all their offspring were grown up and themselves fathers and mothers, had decided to pension her off.

It was Kevin who was the occasion of Roz's next speaking to Mrs Simmons. On warm days, he liked to play tranquil games out on the balcony, talking seriously to himself as he went about his tasks of putting a doll to sleep in its cot, building a lego house, or gently pushing a model car back and forth outside the kitchen window, while inside Roz furiously vacuum-cleaned the bedroom and sitting-room, went on her knees to scrub the kitchen floor, or pounded and rolled the pastry that formed so staple a part of their diet.

Roz looked out of the window, as she always did from time to time when Kevin was playing on the balcony, and there was no sign, no sign at all, of him! Oh, my goodness! She hurried out, hands sticky with pastry, and, having looked to left and right, she went over to the bins. He had been forbidden to go near them, Roz explaining that they were 'dirty' and might well contain such 'nasty things' as maggots, cockroaches and rats. But he was not there, neither behind a bin nor even in one. Then, her heart thumping as it had thumped when she had watched Reg and that white slug-slut go out from the block, cross the yellowing square of squashed seedlings and then clamber, laughing, into the battered old mini, she peered down over the railings. But he was nowhere down there, among the raucous boys in tee-shirts and torn shorts or the knowing girls, one whom was plainly wearing a dress of her mother's, as she minced and wobbled about on what, no less plainly, were her mother's over-large stiletto-heeled shoes.

'Kevin!' she screamed. 'Kevin! Where are you?'

Her voice reverberated, bouncing from wall to wall like that ball that that sixteen-year-old girl with strangely flattened features would hurl tirelessly, hour upon hour, up and down the corridors, until she finally was sent, 'too difficult for us to handle', by her parents to some home so far away in Wales that they could be easy in their consciences if they visited her only once a month.

'Kevin!'

It was then that she saw that the door to Mrs Simmons's lair was slightly ajar. She hurried over, still calling the name.

'Mummy!'

He sounded perfectly happy and safe; and he looked perfectly happy and safe when Roz pushed open the door, not bothering to knock or ring, and came face to face with the old woman, who was holding Kevin by the hand.

'What *are* you doing here?'

'I asked him in for a glass of coca-cola,' the old woman explained in her hoarse, guttural accent, not in the least put out by Roz's accusatory tone and flushed face. It was as though Kevin had mysteriously become her own child and Roz merely his nurse-maid.

Roz never liked Kevin to drink coca-cola, any more than she liked him to suck sweets, having read in some magazine that 'The Home Doctor' regarded sugar as 'the most subtle kind of poison' (that phrase had stuck with her). But she forced herself to smile, as she gasped: 'Oh, what a fright he gave me!'

'Why, what could have happened to him?' The old woman now straightened herself, slowly and with a grimace as though it gave her pain to do so. She then made a gesture with her head. 'Come in!' It was an order; and Roz, though used to orders in the hospital, did not care for one here. But she entered, since she had always been curious about what lay behind those perpetually drawn curtians.

So neat and clean herself, Roz was at first appalled by something that she had hated all her life: mess. It was really to escape mess, as much of rampant emotions as of disorder, dust and dirt, that she had fled that wood-and-cast-iron shack, had vomited ceaselessly aboard that charter plane, and had finally ended up here in Battersea, victim of that remote cousin, her only contact, who had, within days of her arrival, furiously, indefatigably mated with her, had thus fathered Kevin, and had then thrust her out to work, while he himself drank, gambled and peddled drugs. It was mess, too, that she now spent so much of her time clearing up: whether in the hospital, where she was ceaselessly hurrying round with bed-bottles, disinfectant bottles, bedpans and pans and brushes, or here at home, where most of her 'free' hours were spent in scouring and polishing and vacuum-cleaning.

The mess in Mrs Simmons's flat was omnipresent. There was a sweetish smell of it, coming off the grimy curtains and the no less grimy carpets; a sour smell of it breathing from a sink that was cracked, stained and piled high with crockery; an acrid smell of it exhaling from the paraffin-heater which, even on this day of late autumn, was turned so high that it was hardly surprising that the walls themselves were sweating. Boxes, both of tin and cardboard, ancient cabin trunks and suitcases, books and papers were piled higgledy-piggledy everywhere, even on the sofa, chairs and tables. There were blackened pictures – religious, Roz thought rightly, though she did not know that the term for them was icons – on the walls, and among them tattered fragments of lace and brocade pinned here and there, photographs yellowed by time, and two or three sooty portraits in dilapidated frames.

'You'll have some tea?' the old woman said. 'It's made. I always have some ready at this hour.'

Roz nodded, stupefied. Kevin had been clutching a model horse on wheels, coated with dust, and now he began to drag it back and forth across the only bit of floor that was not covered with ill-matching pieces of carpet and rugs. As he tugged at the string, bells tinkled and the horse wagged its tail, not sideways but up and down, as Roz had never seen any horse do before.

There was a samovar, that no doubt had once gleamed in some Russian household but was now almost black from lack of polishing. The old woman went over to a kettle, puffing steam on a gas-ring, took it up with a crocheted holder, and then poured out from it into the samovar. When she had done this, she smiled up at Roz, and suddenly those disconcertingly pale blue eyes, set flat in the face that had the wrinkled, brown appearance of some Indian peasant's, was lit up with a kind of buoyant affection. She took from a shelf a cup without handle and then a saucer with a chip out of it. She blew into the cup, turned it

upside down and shook it, before she held it under the spigot of
the samovar and let the tea drip, like ink, into it.

'Sit, please.'

Roz sat where the old woman indicated on the sofa, even
though it meant that she had to huddle in one corner in order
to avoid a pile of books and a black woollen stocking with a
darning-needle stuck into it. The old woman handed her the
cup. It was difficult to hold it without burning her hands and
eventually she took a handkerchief out of her pocket and
wrapped that around it. She sipped and had to restrain herself
from pulling a face. The tea was as bitter as quinine.

'We've never spoken before.' The old woman stood over her.
'Never.'

'I try to avoid the neighbours. A poor lot. And always
interfering. But I like your little boy. We're good friends. Aren't
we, Kevin?'

With a pang of jealousy, like a sudden constriction of the
muscles round her heart, Roz wondered if, unknown to her,
Kevin had been in here before. Kevin did not reply to the old
woman's question; he did not even look up at the speaking of
his name. The tail of the horse wagged up and down, the bells
tinkled.

'You're not English,' Roz said firmly, as a way of getting her
own back.

The old woman lay down on a daybed in one corner of the
crowded room, kicking off some books, the copy of the Sunday
supplement that she had taken from the dustbin, and a tin tray
decorated with roses in a paint so worn that one could hardly
now make them out. 'No,' she said. 'No. Thank God.'

Roz, who had not been born English either but who had often
wished she had, bridled at that. 'Why "Thank God"?' she asked.

'Dreadful people. No sense of fun. . . . And where do you
come from?'

'The Caribbean,' Roz said, determined not to reveal the name
of her island in an irrational fear that somehow this strange old
woman might use that knowledge against her.

'I wondered if it was that or Africa. Kevin didn't seem to know.'

So Kevin *had* visited here before; she had been right about that! The cheek of it! 'Kevin was born here,' Roz replied with all the dignity that she could muster. 'Well, and what about you? Where are you from?' She did not care if it did not sound polite, even though she had always tried to impress on Kevin the importance of politeness.

'Russia. I say Russia and not the Soviet Union, because there's a difference.'

Again Roz sipped that horrible tea, though she did not want to do so, and again the tail wagged up and down and the bells tinkled.

'Oh, I've lived in almost every corner of the globe,' Mrs Simmons went on. 'In China and in Japan. And in France. Oh, and in Germany. But it seems as if this is where I'm fated to lay down my bones. What a fate! . . . More tea, dear?'

Roz shook her head; she all but shuddered. She gazed about her, her lustrous hair swinging in an arc from side to side. 'You have . . . many things.'

'Yes, many things. I am a rolling stone that has gathered much moss.' Mrs Simmons smiled. 'An exception to the rule. I have always been an exception to every rule.' She added this last sentence with obvious self-congratulation.

Roz pointed to one of the yellowing photographs, in its passe-partout frame. She could make out two horses, a number of dogs and a host of people outside a long, low house. 'Where's that? That's not England.'

'No, that's not England. The Crimea. My old summer home. *One* of my old summer homes. God knows what has happened to it now. The horses dead, the dogs dead, most of the people dead too,' She threw back her head and laughed, and the laugh was a strangely youthful one, coming from that shrivelled, bowed body. She pointed at the photograph. 'I'm there,' she said. Roz peered. 'The girl with the parasol and too much hair and the long nose. *That* one!' She staggered up and placed a far from clean forefinger on one of the figures. 'My looks have improved

with age.' She lay down again on the daybed and then gazed
at Roz with an insolent appraisal, seeming to take in every inch
of her from her springy, shiny hair to the slippers that she had
been wearing when she had rushed out on to the balcony in
search of Kevin. 'You're a handsome woman,' she said at last.
'Don't you have a husband any longer?'

Roz shook her head. She had never had a husband but this
was something that she admitted to no one and would certainly
not admit now to this prying old woman.

'You ought to have a husband. At your age.'

'Men are no good.' Roz spoke from a deep conviction. 'Not
black men. I've learned my lesson.'

'Oh, men are fun, they're fun!' the old woman cried out.
'Black, white or yellow – they're fun!'

Again she gave that astonishingly youthful laugh.

That was how Roz and Mrs Simmons became friends; and that
was how, when Mrs Crombie had to go into hospital for what
she herself described as 'a little op' (in fact, the op proved so big
that she never came out again), Roz began to leave Kevin with
the old woman whenever his hours away from school coincided
with her hours at the hospital. She would still sometimes experience that constriction of the muscles round the heart as she
released the child into that dim-lit lair, with its sagging and
broken pieces of furniture, its grimy walls covered with icons,
portraits, photographs and scraps of lace and brocade, and its
overmastering smell of dust, dissolution and age; but it was better
that he should be there than with those rowdy, raucous children,
their noses snotty and their clothes soiled and tattered, whose
mothers she was always at pains to avoid, not even using the
communal laundry because of them. That same constriction of
the muscles round the heart would make her gasp for breath, the
nostrils of her broad nose flaring, when she would collect him
again and he would whimper at her: 'Oh, not yet, mummy!'
explaining that they were in the middle of a game of beggar-my-
neighbour or were looking at a photograph album.

Often Roz would be persuaded to go in herself, for a cup of acrid tea from that samovar or even for a glass of vodka or wine, poured into a glass so clouded that she would wonder, with distaste, if it had ever been washed since last she had used it. Once, clumsily, she had offered to pay Mrs Simmons for minding Kevin, just as she had paid Mrs Crombie; but the old woman had looked fierce at that, drawing back her lips in a strange kind of snarl as she had snapped: 'Certainly not! Whatever next!' So, instead, Roz got into the habit of doing little jobs for Mrs Simmons.

Such jobs never included any housework; Mrs Simmons adamantly refused to allow that – 'No, no, I can't have anyone touching my things!' But, with the lifts intermittently out of order, the winter advancing, and the old woman often wheezing and barking with bronchitis, Roz was allowed to make journeys for her to the shops or the post office. She received little gratitude. 'Oh, look at these apples you've bought! I said Cox's and any fool can see that these are Golden Delicious!' Mrs Simmons would complain. Or: 'Haven't you any eyes in your head? Half these potatoes are green!' On such occasions, Roz would feel, as she sometimes felt at the hospital, that, because she was black, she was being treated as a menial; but then she reminded herself that Mrs Simmons was old – eighty-eight according to her pension book – and that the old became imperious and crotchety.

Mrs Simmons often interrogated Roz, but she did not herself care to be interrogated.

'Who was Mr Simmons then?'

'A man.'

'Is he dead?'

'Years ago. Thank God.'

'Then is that gentleman who visits you your son by him?'

'No. He's my son but by someone else. And I'm not sure that the word "gentleman" really applies to him.'

'So you've been married twice?'

'I've been married more times than I care to remember.

Simmons was the last. And the worst. I should have known better by then. You *are* being inquisitive, aren't you?'

When the son came to visit the old lady, whether with the friend who looked like a pugilist or without him, Roz and Kevin might have had no existence. Once, as Kevin was playing on the balcony while Roz was washing up at the window, she saw Mrs Simmons and the son (the son's friend was absent) passing on their way to the lift. Kevin looked up at them and then cried out: 'Have you seen my new aeroplane?' Mrs Simmons walked on as though she had never heard him; and it was the son who replied in his bored, languid drawl: 'It looks super.'

The next day, Roz asked Mrs Simmons: 'What does that son of yours do?'

'He writes.'

'Writes? Writes what?'

'Nothing that would be of any interest to you.'

Roz flushed angrily: 'I can read, you know.'

'Yes, dear. And we know *what* you read.'

Yet Mrs Simmons herself was always asking Roz the most intimate of questions; and having first resolved to give away nothing, Roz soon found herself giving away everything. Hers was that kind of nature: money, help, sympathy or merely the information that people asked of her – she could never withhold them. 'Well, you have been a fool!' Mrs Simmons would exclaim, patently gleeful, when she learned something new; or 'Aren't you *ever* going to get any sense into that head of yours?'

Sometimes, very rarely, someone other than the son would call to see Mrs Simmons. There would be a car, usually larger than any ever to be seen on the estate, and on one occasion there was even a chauffeur in one of these cars, with a white moustache and a uniform jacket, the buttons of which were straining over his ample stomach. Mrs Simmons would go down to these cars in a three-quarter-length fur coat and a hat, always the same hat, black with a veil iridescent with tiny spangles, and be driven away for an afternoon or even, on rare occasions, for an afternoon and evening.

'Did you have a nice time?' Roz asked after one of these jaunts.

'Depressing.' Mrs Simmons was lying under a rug on the daybed, her eyes almost closed; and when she heard the question, she had kicked out, a stockinged foot emerging, almost as though she were kicking out at Roz. 'But it was nice to see the lights,' she added, as though repentant for that action. 'There was too much traffic but it was nice to see them.'

After another of these jaunts, the one with the chauffeur at the wheel, Roz had asked: 'Was that lady some relative of yours?' and Mrs Simmons had then answered peevishly: 'Questions! Questions!' before she went on, her voice sharp with sarcasm: 'If it is so important to you to know, she is *not* a relative, not at all! A compatriot.' She pulled a face and then added: 'A thoroughly silly woman.'

Then Mrs Simmons suddenly fell ill. She began to run a temperature, she complained of being 'wobbly' on her legs, and for most of the time she could breathe only with effortful gasps that made the muscles of her neck stand out and her nostrils widen. Roz at last had a pretext to speak to the son, who summoned a doctor. The son, too, behaved towards Roz as though she were some menial; but Roz no longer minded. She had long since got over her jealousy of the old woman's friendship with Kevin, she had become devoted to her – even, at moments of fantasy as she heated up soup or scrambled eggs, imagining that this old woman, bundled up like some ailing bird, all beak and claws, under the rug on the daybed, was her own grandmother, whom she had somehow lost and now at last, all these years later, had found again.

'Dr Cameron's not at all happy about her. But she refuses to come and stay with us and she refuses to go into a home. So what is one to do?'

What one was to do, if one was Roz, was to clean, cook, empty chamber-pots, dash down to the shop, administer pills and prepare inhalations. The inhalations were Roz's own idea, not Dr Cameron's, and Mrs Simmons said that they were the only thing that really helped her. Roz was pleased about that. The smell of eucalyptus and menthol had a strange way of bearing her, like some leaf on an aromatic breeze, back to her childhood in the wood-and-corrugated-iron shack. Kevin would now sit on Mrs Simmons's bed by the hour, playing cards with her when she was strong enough, or else playing by himself when she was not.

One night the old lady was rambling; but she often rambled now, in a twilight state between waking and sleeping, her eyes half shut, so that Roz could only see their whites, and her hands and legs twitching under the bedclothes. 'Oh, that was lovely,' she murmured. 'That really was lovely. You got it right at last. . . .' Roz wondered to what she could be referring; she felt vaguely embarrassed – it was as though she had eavesdropped on something she ought not to have heard.

When Roz went in the next morning to get the old woman her breakfast, she found her, not lying flat, but propped up among cushions from the sofa and the chairs, as well as her pillows. Strewn all over the white crocheted bedspread (only the previous week Roz had washed and ironed it with the utmost care) were innumerable photographs, clearly emptied out of the drawers and suitcases and boxes that were scattered, as though by a burglar, piecemeal about the room. It was extraordinary that someone so frail had been able to lift them. Roz let out a cry of terror: 'What *have* you been doing?'

The old woman did not answer or even move. Her eyes were fixed on something held between both her gnarled hands; and, as she approached, telling herself, but not really believing it, 'This is just one of her moods,' Roz saw that it was one of those strange religious pictures off the wall beside the bed. It showed a Christ on the cross, with a silver halo round his head.

Roz suddenly felt that she was pushing against something that refused to budge; but she went on, pushing and pushing: 'I must hurry. I'm late. Kevin mustn't be late two mornings in a week. Shall I boil you an egg or do you want it scrambled?'

It was a long time before she gave up and realized that the

thing at which she was pushing so frantically would not move.

Everyone ignored Roz, except when there was something to be cleaned or carried or fetched or there was tea or coffee to be made.

'Where's the porter?' the son asked; and then, told, he asked Roz to go down and get him.

'Perhaps I could use your telephone,' he said, and picked up the receiver even before she had answered Yes.

The friend who looked like a pugilist asked about Kevin. Roz said that he was with a neighbour and added that he had not really taken it in that Mrs Simmons had, well, gone for good. But even while she was speaking, the friend had turned away: 'We must find out about the death grant,' he reminded the son.

When the undertakers came to carry away the coffin, Roz suddenly felt, for the first time since she had gone into the bedroom with the dead body propped up there among all those photographs, that she might be about to cry. She asked one of them, an elderly man in a shiny blue-serge suit and with the purple bulbous nose of a chronic drinker, where the funeral would take place; and he replied sternly, 'Putney Vale Crematorium. Strictly private.'

'Oh. I see.' Roz suddenly felt as she had felt when she had leaned over the balcony and watched Reg and that pallid slug-slut with the scarred wrists clamber into the ramshackle mini. 'I'd like to have gone.'

The old man then told her that there was to be a Memorial Service at St Paul's on the Friday after next – 'at 2.15 pip emma'.

'You mean the *cathedral*?' Roz was astounded.

The old man laughed, shaking his head as he rubbed one side of that purple, bulbous nose with a forefinger. 'No, not the cathedral,' he said. 'St Paul's in Covent Garden.'

Roz dressed Kevin up in the grey pin-stripe suit, with short trousers and long dark grey worsted stockings, that she had specially bought for the occasion. She herself wore a dark blue dress and a dark blue hat with a wide brim that dipped low over her forehead, also specially bought.

The journey by bus was a long one, involving a number of changes, and during it Kevin became increasingly fretful and Roz became increasingly irritated with him. She had found the church on a map lent to her by one of the male nurses, a Portuguese, at the hospital; but it was far harder to find in reality. So it was that it was long past '2.15 pip emma' when, a whimpering Kevin tugged along behind her, she at last hurried up the steps.

To her amazement, it was totally impossible to enter the church. It was so crowded that there were even a number of people massed in the doorway. Roz could hear a voice, reverberant and solemn, but, even when she stood on tiptoe and craned her neck to its full extent, she could not see the speaker. A tall, fidgety man in a dark blue velvet suit, who had kept touching his cloud of soft blond hair with one hand as she had attempted to peer round his shoulder, now tut-tutted when she made a lunge to push past.

'Sorry,' Roz whispered.

At that moment Kevin trod on the toecap of one of the man's highly polished brogues. 'Christ!'

'Sorry,' Roz whispered again, since clearly Kevin was not going to apologize. Then she asked: 'Is this the Memorial Service for Mrs Simmons?' She felt sure that there must be some mistake.

The man nodded impatiently. 'Yes – for Irina Akinievna. Mrs Simmons.' He pursed his lips and again his hand fluttered to that cloud of soft, blond hair. Clearly he wanted no more conversation, as, invisible, a choir began to sing 'The Lord is my shepherd . . .' and Kevin simultaneously set up a monotonous keening, not of grief but of boredom and tiredness.

'But such a crowd. . . . So many people. . . .' Roz stammered. 'How . . . how is it possible?'

The young man darted her a contemptuous look, tossed his

head, and gave a fastidious shudder. 'Well,' he said, 'she used to get audiences twenty times this size at the Coliseum.'

It was only then that Roz began to realize that the old woman must once have been famous; and only much later that she discovered that, along with Pavlova and Karsavina, she had been one of the three greatest ballerinas of her generation.

F

Appetites

To the high, gleaming catafalque at one end of the ward they all bore their offerings. Come my treasure, my little doll, my little bird, eat, eat, *eat*. That was Aunt Sotiria, who was not really an aunt but a distant cousin, the arthritic joints of her fingers swollen as though from the constriction of her many knobbly rings, stooping over Maria and pleading. But I made these *dolmadakia* myself, try one, just a single bite, a single little bite. The *dolmadakia*, as lumpy as her fingers, lay piled one on top of the other in a grey plastic box filched from the disordered kitchen of one of the many disordered women, wives of television producers, journalists or publishers, for whom she cleaned and cooked in Camden Town. She tilted the box and an emerald slime, collecting in a corner, glittered evilly. Eat, eat, eat.

Uncle Kostas, who was not really an uncle but also a distant cousin, related to Aunt Sotiria by a nexus of relationships as tenuous and tough as a spider's web, suggested all the delicacies that he thought might coax Maria's appetite. *Taramasalata*, just a little of it, spread on a cracker? A salt herring, a salt herring was the best cure for nausea, he knew that from his days, oh many years ago, on the Athens–Crete run. Or how about some liver, thinly sliced and fried for a few seconds in the finest olive oil? There was nothing easier for the stomach to digest than liver. Now the two of them, the aunt and the uncle who were really only distant cousins, each leant over Maria, their faces vaguely affronted and uncomprehending at her lack of all response.

Soon Takis, another cousin, who was studying mechanical engineering at the North London Polytechnic, joined them with his English girl-friend, Sue. At first Sue remained indifferent, huddled into a coat of simulated fur which, hands deep in pockets, she kept wrapped tightly around her plump body as though she were hugging herself in self-congratulation at having such a healthy appetite. Come my treasure, my little doll, my little bird, eat, eat, *eat*. Takis used the same words but gave them a slightly hectoring edge. He had brought a round wooden box of *loukoumia*, with a little wooden fork that he jabbed into the gelatinous, pink-powdered cube that seemed largest to him. Come, come. He was a handsome boy, with a high-bridged nose and thick, arched eyebrows above it. He smelled of Greek cigarettes, pungent as burning hay, and of the hair oil, sweetly sickly, that gleamed in a line on his forehead where the black, curly hair sprang upwards. He held out the cube on its fork and fragments of pinkish sugar drifted down, a sunset snowfall, on to the pillow. Sue roused herself, her protuberant, previously vacant eyes focusing themselves on the catafalque. You must eat, you know. You have to force yourself. Once you've started again, you'll find it easier and easier. That was how the nurses also spoke to Maria. They felt sorry for her, one couldn't help feeling sorry for her, so fragile and so pretty and so undemanding, but they also felt exasperated. There was even a Nigerian nurse, with a high bosom like a bolster, who told her that among her people there were children who starved not by choice but because there was no food for them. Sue got up and approached the catafalque. I'm not surprised that that Turkish Delight turns her off. What she needs is some fruit. Grapes. Or a banana. Or a nice crisp Cox's. She was now speaking as though the girl on the catafalque could either not hear her or not understand her. But Takis again extended the gelatinous pink cube and again the sunset snowfall drifted downwards.

Widowed Kyria Papadopoulou arrived, her wide-hipped, deep-bosomed body balanced miraculously on the slimmest of legs, the most fragile of ankles, the highest of heels. She owned the City restaurant at which Maria had been working. Her son, whom she henpecked as she had once henpecked his father,

served as her chef. I've brought you a chicken-wing, I know you
like chicken as my Petros does it. The skin is all crisp, see, and
there's just the faintest flavour of *rigani*. Come my treasure, my
little doll, my little bird, eat, eat *eat*. She tore at the chicken with
long, red-lacquered fingernails and held out a sliver. Come,
come, *come*! Then, rejected, she turned away with a shrug of
plump shoulders under her coat of real, not simulated, fur.
What's the matter with the child? What's one to do? She too
spoke as though the girl on the catafalque could either not hear
her or not understand her.

Eventually they all forgot the girl, the reason for their visit,
and, ranged in a semicircle about the catafalque, started themselves to devour the food they had brought.

Kyria Papadopoulou, please try these home-made *dolmadakia*.
I am sure you have better in your famous restaurant but please
try one, please.

Some chicken, Sue? Try some of Kyria Papadopoulou's
chicken. I bet you've never eaten anything like it.

What would really tempt me is just the teeniest bit of that
Turkish Delight. I don't usually like it. My figure. But. (A gelatinous fragment glued itself to one of Sue's front teeth, softly
pink on its enamelled hardness.)

I was saying a salt herring. *Taramasalata*.

Fried liver.

Well, just another teeniest, weeniest piece.

Plenty of chicken here.

The girl on the catafalque stared motionless up at the ceiling.
Soon a sister trotted up, like a mettlesome, broad-beamed pony.
I really must ask you. Too much noise here. Disturbing the other
patients. Some of them very sick. Shouldn't really be so many of
you. Only two at a time.

When at last all of them had gone (I'll leave the *loukoumia* here,
you may be tempted later), it seemed only a few moments before
the Nigerian nurse rattled up with a tray. Now then, dear, you
won't have any difficulty in getting this lot down. She peered

enviously into the still open, round wooden box. Fancy bringing you sweets like that. Silly. (In her flat, beyond the Archway, her mother was minding her infant son; that Turkish Delight would be just the present for them.) There's a simple broth here, can't upset you, and a macaroni cheese and a nice milk pudding. But Maria turned her head away, with a gasp and a little groan. The Nigerian nurse banged down the tray (Well, please yourself, she thought but did not say) and hurried off to attend to another patient. She hadn't got all day, take it or leave it, she wasn't going to be late off duty yet again.

By now the restaurant would have started to fill. I could do with a real good blow-out. Well, you'll get that here. There's not much finesse in the way things are served but for value for money. Sweat on flushed foreheads. Saliva in the rubbery folds of mouths. Phew! Teeth tear at the leg of a duck, grease dribbling down a chin. Glutinous rice is piled on to a fork. A roll bears a smear of lipstick as though it were blood. Maria! I say, Maria! A fist like a ham splashes greenish oil from a cracked bottle on to a heap of plump courgettes. Some more of this vino, Maria. To your very good health. Poured gurgling from dusty demi-johns into carafes that look like hospital bottles, the wine (red to the English customers, black to Maria) seems to clot on the, tongue, its first sweetness sharpening to acid. Maria, be an angel, some more butter! In this heat the yellow trails of butter on the dish are deliquescent. A fork whirls a fragment of bread round and round in a pungent orange sauce. A mouth opens, closes, masticates with grunts and snorts. An American woman's voice, metallic and high: If I eat another morsel, I'll just throw up! Truly I will. Nonsense! You must try these profiteroles. Speciality of the *maison*. Out of this world. Fabulous. Maria! Maria my sweet! Where are you? *Parakalo!* (On a previous visit he had asked her how to say 'please' in Greek.) In the kitchen Petros puts a finger into the mayonnaise, takes it out, licks it. Too much vinegar, he scolds an underling. I've told you before. The underling ladles the mayonnaise out over some cold fish, indifferent to the criticism. Maria!

The girl on the catafalque still lay out motionless. Not eating, love? It was the woman on her right, shapeless and friendless, who habitually devoured Maria's food as well as her own, as though by sating the monster greedily and mortally at work within her, she could somehow appease it and lull it to sleep. Maria did not answer and the woman crept out of bed, a famished and furtive cat, and quickly exchanged her empty try for the girl's full one. Waste not, want not. She had fed five children (two dead now) first from the breast and then from the meagre sums doled out to her by a drunkard husband. Now she fed herself with the same desperate, obsessive persistence.

Maria closed her eyes, open so long on the bare, white ceiling.
    . . . Now she is back in her native Cyprus, in the village that no longer exists, minding the sheep that no longer exist on some rocky hillside or in some barren ravine. The sheep are thin, she is thin. The year has been a bad one, first ruinous storms, then a summer-long drought. She is hungry, she is often hungry, but she puts off the moment when she will unwrap the piece of newspaper that lies at the bottom of the tasselled bag slung over her shoulder. Not yet. No, not yet. She can hold out another ten minutes, fifteen minutes, half an hour. The bread is hard and coarse; she might be chewing on some friable excrescence plucked from the rocks sticking up all around her. The *feta* cheese might not be cheese at all but a slab of chalk as it crumbles in her mouth. Both are miraculously clean and astringent. She bites into a pear, her strong white teeth crunching on its strong white flesh. Juice trickles down her chin and on to the palm of her hand, following the dirt-seamed cracks. She bites again. The pear is gravid with the thick, musky summer air. She gets up, wiping her hands down on the coarse black folds of her skirt, and begins to leap downwards from rock to rock, the sheep baaing and blathering around her. There is a spring at the bottom of the ravine, oozing out from a dark jagged mouth with a beard of emerald moss. The water is ice-cold and clear. Clean. She cups it in her hands, lowers her head, gulps. The water

tingles on her tongue and behind her nose. It seems to tingle in her brain, clearing spaces there until it seems as light as an empty honeycomb.

Cocoa, dear? The nurse who now approached the catafalque had recently begun to resent Maria after some days of feeling affectionate and protective towards her. She won't respond, I hate patients who will simply make no effort. She was a nurse who took each death as a personal affront to her; who bored her flat mates by bringing the hospital, with its stinks, agonies and bereavements, into their own heedless, happy-go-lucky lives; who ordered her patients 'Now recover!' and expected them to obey her.

Maria gulped, turned aside her head.

No?

No.

The psychiatrist, a dumpy middle-aged woman with stumpy fingers, wearing a leather jacket that had the sheen of pork crackling to it and a woollen skirt of the texture and colour of curdled milk, sat down, lumpy legs wide apart, beside the catafalque. Her eyes, palest of blue irises surrounded by a liverish yellow that looked like mutton fat, brooded on the girl. What to say?

Any better, dear?

Haven't you been able to force yourself to eat even the smallest bite?

The Viennese accent reminded Maria of the cake shop in Golders Green to which the Swedish boy, met at the language school, used to take her. There were éclairs that oozed a puslike custard, chocolate cakes of a glistening blackness that suggested, suggested . . . Better not to think of them.

Is something on your mind?

Repeat that: Maria, is something on your mind? Try to answer me, dear.

A shake of the head.

Home-sick?

Shake.

Love-sick?

Shake.

Life-sick?

Shake.

The psychiatrist's stomach rumbled mournfully, a tube train shuddering deep in the bowels of the earth. It had been a long day and she looked forward to sitting down with her friend to a pot of tea, scrambled eggs on toast, Danish pastries, the telly. She might stop by at the deli and buy some smoked salmon as a treat. Be extravagant. One had to spoil oneself now and then.

You do awfully little to help yourself, you know, my dear.

It was not what a psychiatrist was supposed to say; but after a long day, when she was hungry and felt the first premonitory throb of a headache, the words came unbidden.

No one can help you if you don't help yourself. (Kyria Papadopoulou had told Maria, when she had first come to work in the restaurant: Now, Maria, whenever you feel you want to eat something, just help yourself. Kyria Papadopoulou had been kind.) That's the lesson we all have to learn.

But Maria was beyond learning lessons.

The psychiatrist got to her feet, tugging down that shapeless skirt the colour and texture of curdled milk and buttoning up that leather jacket that had the sheen of pork crackling. Well, dear, I'll come by again tomorrow. And before that I want you to do something for me. Will you do something for me? Maria?

Maria stared at the ceiling, which was as hard and smooth as the icing of one of Petros's wedding cakes.

Maria?

No answer.

I want you to do something for me. A favour. A special, a very special favour.

Eat.

EAT.

Motionless on the catafalque in the darkened ward, her neighbour
grunting and snoring and sometimes emitting a strange, whinny-
ing cry beside her, Maria dreamed.

There are huge, shark-like mouths, the teeth murderously
serrated, and the saliva loops down from them in shiny ropes.
The teeth masticate with a crackling and crunching. Blood
spurts, arrow-heads of bone fly out in all directions. Marrow
squelches. Sounds of gulping, slurping, choking, eructation.
Maria, bring me. Bring me. More. Another. A plate of. A bottle
of. Do you call this a helping? A long tongue unrolls itself
around a finger smeared with a mud-like chocolate. A toothpick
probes a gigantic molar in which a sliver of chicken nestles, a
glistening mollusc in its shell. Bite. Chew. Swallow. Belch.

Oh, no, I can't, can't, can't!

The night nurse, a little Filippino with wide, startled eyes,
hurried out.

What's the matter?

Oh, no, no, no!

The neighbour stirred from a dream of a delicious pork pie.
Fancy waking everyone in the ward. Does it night after night.
Ought to be in a loony bin.

Now, Maria, swallow this pill.

Swallow.

NO!

They gave up trying to wheedle, coax and bully. There were
tubes of plastic and rubber, coiled like intestines. There were
syringes that looked like the implements used by Petros to ice
his cakes. Maria threw herself about, the hands that had first
gently restrained her growing impatient and brutal. She wailed
in protest. She thrashed like a landed fish. That'll tranquillize
her. There was sweat on the doctor's forehead, glistening like
that sickly-sweet hair oil on Takis's. He might have been a diner
at the restaurant, overheated with too much food and drink.
Stupid cow, he muttered. It was not what a doctor, even one so
young, was supposed to say. But he had been to a party the

night before, he had quarrelled with his girl-friend, each time
that he exerted himself, it was as though a mallet were thumping
down on the back of his head. The Nigerian nurse's arms were
more muscular than his. If you'd be sensible and eat, you'd
save yourself and us a lot of trouble. The needle homed deep.

But just as her mouth and her teeth and her tongue and her
throat and her stomach rebelled, so now even the cells of her
ever-diminishing, ever-dwindling body rebelled and refused
inexplicably to feed on what the young, sweating, red-faced
doctor and his assistants gave them. I dunno. Can't understand
it. No response. Weird. The grey, world-weary consultant did
not know either; but he was able to find some elaborate scientific
synonyms for his ignorance.

Even when she weighed less than five stone and was so light
that the Nigerian nurse could have rocked her in her brawny
arms as she rocked her infant son, Maria's beauty, so far from
withering, seemed only to blossom further. Even the young
doctor, with his bloodshot eyes and his throbbing morning head,
noticed it. Walking away from her down the long white corridor
in his lisping suède bootees, he is all at once trailing, a small boy,
behind his doctor father and an obesely waddling spaniel dog on
the downs behind their Brighton home. Under the bushes he
sees a bone, violin-shaped, chalk-white with tinges here and
there of emerald. He picks it up with his nail-bitten fingers,
turns it over and over, stares down at it. It is hard, clean and
pure. It is beautiful. He wants to take it home with him. But his
father turns impatiently and calls, Oh come *on*! And then his
father wanders back, followed by the dog, and asks: What on
earth have you got there? A bone, he says, just a bone. His
father takes it from him. A rabbit's head, he says. I should think.
Or a cat's. Anyway, we don't want to play around with something like that. Unhygienic. An arm swings, the miniature white
violin glitters momentarily in the sun. Then it is lost. The boy
wants to cry but he knows the kind of voice, contemptuous and
cold, in which his father will demand, *Now* what are you
blubbing about? So he runs ahead. The dog stays with his father.

The bone, hard, clean and pure, lay out on the catafalque. He stared down at it and again, as so many years before, he wanted to cry. But someone – perhaps the grey, world-weary consultant or the Nigerian nurse with the high bosom like a bolster – would ask him, *Now* what are you blubbing about? and he didn't want that to happen. So he hurried away down the corridor, his suède bootees lisping on the highly polished floor.

That day they closed the restaurant.

I loved her like a daughter, Kyria Papadopoulou said. It's the least I can do for her now. She had never had a daughter of her own, much though she had wanted one; and though she nagged incessantly at Petros to marry this or that girl that she found for him, he, so obedient in every other respect, remained inexplicably recalcitrant in that.

Why, why, why? cried Aunt Sotiria.

Why? They all took it up.

Home-sick?

Love-sick?

Life-sick?

They all had their indefatigably voracious appetites; they were bewildered and abashed by her loss of hers.

Uncle Kostas sobbed noisily at the funeral, thinking of a wife coughing out her lungs in the starved years of the Occupation, of a daughter bleeding to death in childbirth and a son swallowed up, and therefore as good as dead, in the insatiable maw of the New World, of comrades shot by Germans or their fellow countrymen, lost at sea, crushed on high roads, burned by fevers in the crowded wards of hospitals. Kostas bit his lower lip until he thought it would bleed. Petros wondered if the cake, a marvel of the confectioner's art, had been taken out of the refrigerator by his snotty underling. Sue twitched her coat of simulated fur closer about her, peered disdainfully into the newly dug grave and wished that she could afford a coat of real fur, expensive fur, like that old trout's over there.

Back at the restaurant they huddled for a while around the

cast-iron stove, holding out fingers mauve with cold and feeling the skin of their faces tauten and tingle. Then, bit by bit, their desolation melted from them, as their dully aching bodies thawed out. Petros hurried into the kitchen and they could hear his voice, high-pitched and nasal, upbraiding the snotty underling. I told you. Why didn't you turn down the gas? I told you. Why didn't you open the wine? I told you. Why didn't you take the cake out of the refrigerator?

But everyone agreed that it was a wonderful spread. Kyria Papadopoulou always did you proud. She spared no expense, you'd have to go far to find a cook as good as her Petros. They slurped from bowls of steaming *avgolemono* soup. They tore at the fresh-baked rolls and shoved chunks of them into their mouths, so that Sue, one cheek crammed, looked as though she had toothache. They picked up the lamb chops in their fingers and their teeth tugged at them, while fat dribbled down their chins and even on to the *broderie Anglaise* of Aunt Sotiria's crisply starched blouse. They drained their glasses, their mouths leaving messy imprints on their rims, and, as soon as they had done so, Uncle Kostas would at once brandish yet another bottle and pour out from it, spattering the clean linen cloth as though with blood. Petros, usually so ladylike, picked up a *keftedaki* in his fingers and rammed it between his teeth. His mother sighed, belched, muttered, Excuse me, and settled herself yet more deeply in her chair, her plump elbows resting on the table with the dishes all around them. There were other relatives, other friends, other people whom no one really knew, all guzzling, swigging, gulping, sozzling.

Suddenly, with a shooting pain under the heart like a stab of indigestion, Aunt Sotiria was transfixed by the thought of Maria, their own little Maria, lying out there in the dark and cold, the earth heavy upon her lightness. Tears began to roll unchecked down her cheeks, even while she was intent on gnawing at the leg of a chicken.

What is it, Sotiria *mou*? Uncle Kostas asked.

Crunch, crackle, suck.

What is it? What is it?

That child. That poor child.

Ah, Maria! Kyria Papadopoulou's face became tragic as she ladled out more of the *stifado* on to her plate.

Maria!

Sue murmured, Poor darling, as she picked out a fragment of meat from between her front teeth with red-lacquered fingernail.

How she loved Petros's cakes! Kyria Papadopoulou groaned, as much from the weight of her grief as from that of the food that was now lying heavy on her stomach.

I took a cake to the hospital for her, Petros said, nodding his head sadly, but she was so ill she wouldn't eat a slice. The other patients had it all. I hadn't the heart to bring it back.

Uncle Kostas got shakily to his feet, his grizzled hair in a tangle over his forehead and his face all flushed and sweaty, as though he had been running a race. Let us drink, he said and raised his glass high. Let us drink to the memory of Maria, our little Maria!

Maria!

Maria!

Our little Maria!

Sue's pointed fingernail eased a cherry off the cake, causing Petros to squint in anger. She popped the cherry into her mouth and then she too said, Maria!

If only she could be here eating this feast with us now, Aunt Sotiria cried.

If only!

Oh, if only!

The snotty underling, breathing asthmatically through his perpetually open mouth, tottered in, to the cheers of the whole assembly, with a sucking pig on a vast platter awash with grease. It weighed even more than the body in the cemetery.

Voices

IN the years of dubious fame, of fretful travel, of the hours spent in the heat of television studios or the chill of laboratories, lying alone or lying in the arms of Krishna, Pearl would always remember the exact moment when she first knew that she could do It. A duckling takes to the water, a nestling takes to the air. A moment of doubt, followed by a moment of terror; and then the new element embraces her as though she had entered it a hundred times already. . . .

A child of eight, in the summer dawn, Pearl stands, nacreously pallid and gleaming in her nightdress, behind the net curtain of her attic window. There is sweat on her forehead and her bare arms. There is sun already in the long narrow garden, that same sun that day after day has made her feel enervated and listless; but during the night (or did she imagine it?) she heard the far-off rumble of thunder, as though some giant's hammer were beating on the ground. She yawns, she watches, one fragile hand lifting a corner of the curtain. The two women, her mother and her aunt, also in their nightdresses, walk together down the garden, their arms linked; and dark on the dew-sprinkled grass their footsteps melt and merge. They are going down to the orchard and as they sway and sidle, their plump bodies colliding with each other, unresisting flesh against unresisting flesh, their heads bend towards each other. But from high up here, under the steeply sloping roof that retains the heat of the day all through the restless nights, Pearl cannot hear what they are saying to each other. Her mother's hair is a jet, gipsy black; Aunt Marion's is streaked with grey, hanging loose down a neck that

has a little creased cushion of fat just above the shoulder blades.
Pearl imagines the swish of their nightdresses as they make their
way from the close-shaven lawn (yesterday her father had at
last been bullied into mowing it) into the long, wet grass of
the orchard as though they were wading arm-in-arm into a
shallow sea. Pearl knows where they are going. Against the far
wall, crumbling like one of those dry sponge cakes that Aunt
Marion makes for tea, stand the peach trees, their branches
heavy with fruit. The women approach them, loosening their
hold on each other as though they were nearing some mystery
or rite. The sun glimmers along an upraised arm. That is Aunt
Marion, tiptoeing up as she plucks the huge ripe peach from
one of the highest branches. For several days she has marked
it down and waited, patient yet persistent. Pearl's mother now
goes up on tiptoe too and feels, feels, feels among the fruit, her
fingers wary not to bruise or pluck until she is sure that the
precise moment has come. Pearl leans out, the ledge of the high
window pressing against her flat, bony chest. Sweat beads her
upper lip and, when she runs her tongue along it, it tastes salt
and brackish.

There has been a strange, aimless kind of languor in all the
women's movements as each has plucked a fruit; but now, with
impetuous greed, they bite into the flesh, the juice running down
their chins and staining their nightdresses. Aunt Marion squints
up at her sister, the rising sun stabbing at her weak-sighted eyes
behind their gold-framed glasses; the glasses catch fire. Mother
says something and both women laugh. If only she, Pearl,
glimmering high above their heads at the window of the attic
bedroom, could hear them! She is always conscious of this secret
world of theirs, in which the languorous plucking of the peaches
is only yet another rite from which they exclude her. If only . . .
Then all at once the duckling takes to the water, the nestling
takes to the air. A moment of doubt, followed by a moment of
terror; and then she *can* hear them. . . .

There's nothing else for it. (Aunt Marion flings the peach stone
from her into the long grass.)

Yes but. (Mother is again on tiptoe, reaching among the leaves, jumps, yanks.)

You've got to face. (Aunt Marion also reaches up, feels, rejects, feels again.)

But the child, for her sake.

She'll come to far more harm if you stick with him.

Yes but.

He's never been any good to you and he never will be.

Oh but.

No, Eileen, never any good at all.

Well but.

Run through your money, made a slave of you, can't hold down a job.

Yes but.

Half-cut most of the time, lazy, hopeless, hopeless, hopeless.

Pearl could now even hear the disgusting champing noises of their teeth, the salivation and the sucking of the juice, as they wolfed, talked, wolfed. But she no longer wanted to hear. She had heard enough. She ran back to the bed, jumped into it and pulled first the sheet and then the pillow over her head. But the voices went on.

Got to face up to it.

Oh but.

Not fair to the child, not fair to yourself. It's now or never. Leave him.

Yes if only.

There's no if only about it. Tell him this morning. That's my girl. Just as soon as he comes out of that drunken sleep of his. Tell him.

Oh, Marion.

Tell him.

However tight she pulled the pillow over her head and however deep she burrowed down under the sheet, she could not stop hearing. She had launched herself into the new element and now, carried out on the long, brimming tide, the hot upward thrust of air impelling her pinions forward, she could not escape from it.

2

That was when she first knew that she could do It. Soon, she was to learn that she sometimes did It without wishing to do It; and soon, too, that it was better not to let anyone, not even Mother and Aunt Marion, know that she could do It.

They leave that house and years later Pearl's only recollection of the place is of a cramped attic bedroom, a window so high that its ledge presses against her flat, bony chest and two women, at the start of a summer day, leaving a dark trail behind them on silvery grass and then reaching up, with languorous movements, to pluck the ripe peaches from the trees at the far end of a rankly overgrown garden. There was a man in the house, who was often described as 'ill' and whom Pearl would often be forbidden to approach in the study in which he spent so many of his hours since he had ceased to go out to work. He had been a jolly man, once, long ago, and he could still be jolly, even if with a jolliness that made Aunt Marion and Mother watch him warily, drawing in their breaths with a sharp hiss when his fun became too strident; but the jolliness of those last months seldom lasted, petering out in an aftermath of sulks and headaches or exploding in an orgy of shouts and broken crockery. Sometimes he would hold Pearl close to him, his breath heavy with the smell of pipe smoke and that other mysterious smell that she so much hated; and Mother or Aunt Marion would then order him to let the girl be, it was disgusting, the poor wee thing, had he no shame? I'll do what I bloody well please in my own house, he would yell, flinging the child from him; and Mother, icy and acid, would then query, Your own house?

Well, whoever owned the house, they leave it, first for a smaller one in a meaner suburb; and then for a flat, damply cavernous, in a mansion block south of Clapham Common.

Coming home from school, as she watches the bus approaching, Pearl has a sensation of gentle pressure inside her forehead

and a sensation of a wind blowing against her fragile throat; and
she is doing It, without wanting to do It. She can hear the two
women, who at that moment are drinking their dark, bitter tea
together two miles away, a letter open on the table between them.

He says there it's a death sentence.

Don't you believe it, it's nothing but a bid for sympathy.

But the doctor.

Who knows if he's ever seen any doctor at all?

But cirrhosis.

It's no more than he deserves.

Yes, but I feel.

Now you don't want to get mixed up with him again, after
you've managed to get free.

Oh, but one can't help.

Think of Pearl . . .

Perhaps they are thinking of Pearl, shimmeringly nacreous
schoolgirl, for then there is a silence; and Pearl, seated alone on
the top of the bus, is thinking of them and of the father who used
to hold her so tight against his chest as he breathed over her those
fumes of pipe smoke and alcohol. He is dying? In need? On his
own? She longs to be with him. Smooth his sheet. Carry a tray
and tell him, It's such a lovely day outside. Take his temperature.
She longs to hear his voice. But try though she may, a vein
throbbing, throbbing, throbbing at a corner of her foreheead
somehow she cannot do It. Perhaps he is too far for her to rach,
him.

She runs down the street from the bus stop and dashes into
the house. What's all the hurry about? Aunt Marion asks; and
Mother, slipping the letter under the tablecloth, says, You must
have known that your auntie had baked one of her cakes. (The
yellow wall crumbles in the early morning sunshine behind the
peach trees; the peaches are gravid with juice.) Pearl cries out,
Is he ill? I want to go to him. Where is he? Why didn't you tell
me? The two women look at each other in shock and astonish-
ment and then they both look at her in anger.

You've no business to eavesdrop.

And how did you get away from school so early?

Pretending to have just rushed in off the bus and all the time. I've told you before.

All this hanging about outside closed doors listening to things that are no concern of yours.

Let this be the last time.

But I. Pearl does not continue. She knows that she must never, ever tell them that she can do It.

Yet slowly the women guess; and it frightens them, so that they never dare to put it into words to each other. Such a funny little thing. (Aunt Marion creams the butter and sugar with frowning concentration.) Almost as though she could read one's thoughts. One can't hide anything from her, Mother agrees, woefully totting up figures (electricity, gas, rates) on the back of an envelope that contains another of his scrawled, pleading letters (even a quid or two would help). It's quite creepy, it really is. So artful.

He dies at last; and though Aunt Marion tells Mother, I shouldn't say anything about it to her, why upset her, what's the point? she hears them from far away in the baker's shop where she has gone to buy a loaf and she rushes into the house and screams, Why didn't you let me see him? Why didn't you? Just once, only once! And now I'll never see him again! The two women look stricken and frightened and, more to her sister and herself than to the child, Aunt Marion commands, Now pull yourself together.

3

Krishna became their lodger two or three years after that. He came between the Turk whom Aunt Marion had to ask to leave because he wet his bed and the Arab who used to try to fondle Pearl's nascent breasts whenever he found himself alone with her. (This is our secret. You must never tell your Mummy and your auntie, Bearl. He could never pronounce a P.) Krishna was beautiful, pliant and sickly, like some exotic plant, perhaps a plant from his own native India, that stands in a northern sitting-room with its weak branches reaching out towards the distant sun; but the core of the plant was extraordinarily fibrous and resilient. His was the attic room opposite hers and he had it strewn with the components that he used for his work. He was a student, on some kind of scholarship, at Imperial College, but he was far cleverer than any of his fellow-students, Pearl was sure of that. His palms, when he took both her hands in his hands, were strangely soft and cool. He wore a gold bracelet round one girlish wrist. His shoulder-length hair swung from side to side when he was working at his table. If she shut her eyes as she touched that hair, it felt exactly as if she were touching grass. He had a small beaky nose, as of some bird of prey, and huge eyes, ringed as with bruises, that seemed to look deep inside her and plumb her secret from that first moment that they met. He knew at once that she could do It. She had never had to tell him.

It could be hyperaesthesia, he speculated in his soft sing-song voice.

Hyper what?

He explained. There was Gilbert Murray. He would go to the other end of the house and then, when he was summoned back, he would know what people had been saying.

But this isn't just the other end of the house. Or even the other end of the street. It can be, oh, miles.

He smirked; he did not really believe her when she said that; he thought she was boasting, in the way that children do. (After all, she was only fourteen.) But he began patiently to test her, forcing her to concentrate while she felt that increasing pressure within her forehead and that wind that, on the stillest day, blew against her throat; and miraculously she would tell him what her aunt had been saying to her mother or what he had been saying to either of them while she had been far away at school or at the shops or in the park. He was puzzled then, as the doctor had been puzzled when for several days she had run a temperature without any other symptom. He would look at her, with a wondering insistence, sometimes holding both her hands in his (the palms so cool, so soft) and he would tell her, You're an odd one, without a doubt.

But I don't want to be odd. I just want to be normal.

You can't help it. Can you? That's how you're made.

Oh but.

You're a very exceptional person, Pearl. The whole world will be interested in you. You'll see.

4

Now the whole world is interested in her. At first Mother has doubts about it. You don't want to be a freak, you don't want to be like something in a fun-fair. But this nacreous freak earns money and her fun-fair is the world. There are articles about her in the newspapers. She appears on the television, the two plump sisters leaning hungrily towards her flickering image as countless people are doing the whole length and breadth of the country. Other children claim to have the same power, but of course they haven't. She spends several weeks at an American university, Krishna always with her. There are articles about her in the journals of Psychic Research. Her photograph appears on the covers of two Sunday Supplements simultaneously. She feels perpetually tired, as though she were bleeding, on and on and on, from an invisible wound. But she owes it to science and to herself to continue with the experiments, Krishna tells her; and she knows that she also owes it to Krishna, whom she has come to love, and to her mother and her aunt, who no longer have to take in lodgers and who have moved from Clapham to Chelsea. Krishna tells her and anyone else who is interested that she has taken a step ahead of the rest of the human race in the process of evolution. Some day, sooner or later, everyone will be able to do It. But since for the moment she alone has the capability, she must endure all this travel, all these questions, all these tests, all these people, all this tiredness.

She becomes pregnant while on a visit to Zürich. This is something that Krishna, who plans everything for her, did not plan; but he is always businesslike and, telling her that nothing must be allowed to get in the way of their 'work' – later, he says, of course they will get married – he arranges for her to go into a clinic, one of the most expensive in Switzerland if not in the world, and the foetus is removed from her. Has It somehow been removed with the foetus? She does not know; she is really too tired to think clearly about it. But there is the fact, which she and Krishna must face together in the burnished Zürich laboratory: humiliatingly she can no longer do It. Soon there will be an article in a Swiss scientific journal to say that under stringent conditions the subject was totally unable to produce any phenomena at all. In the overheated, luxury hotel Krishna shouts at her, You stupid cow. What's the matter with you? Why don't you try? She feels totally drained of blood. It must have all flowed away, a black, sticky river, when their child was ripped from her.

Well, never mind, we'll have to think of something. Krishna is, after all, a genius in his own way. True, he can't hear what people are saying unless they are in earshot but his professor did say that he was one of the most promising students ever to have come to him from India. Krishna works hard in the work room that he has at the top of the Chelsea house, while Pearl sits watching the television with the two sisters, who, sensing that she can no longer do It, for the first time for many years feel a sense of community with the nacreously pallid child-woman.

After many weeks Krishna produces an electrode about the size of a penny, which is covered on its operative surface with a thin film of mylar. He tells the bewildered Pearl that they are going to Barcelona where a cousin of his practises as a dentist. The cousin is, in fact, the husband of a second cousin; and though he is a good dentist, he has found few patients in the country of his exile and has many debts.

But I don't need a dentist.

Krishna says something about her needing 'prosthetic dentistry'. She has no idea what this can mean. Trust me, he says; and though he is the least trustworthy of men, she trusts him because she loves him. It is only in the Barcelona hotel that he tells her, a soft and cool palm sliding over her fragile forearm, that he and the dentist are going to give It back to her.

What do you mean?

He explains but, since she is not very bright, she has difficulty in understanding him. An element for receiving electromagnetic signals at radio frequency. Transducer element coupled with receiving element and with live nerve ending of a tooth. Electromagnetic signals converted to electric signals at audio frequency for transmission to the brain.

But I don't understand all this! And I don't want all this!

Perfectly simple. You wouldn't want to have to sell the house, now would you? Turn out mother and auntie? And how otherwise can we ever get married and have the baby that we want? Won't hurt. Easiest thing in the world to operate once you get used to it. Tongue like this. (He demonstrates, pressing a long, sinuous tongue against a molar, mouth ajar. Horrified, she peers into the crimson cavern.) Tongue presses against exposed terminal on back tooth. The amazingly soft and cool palm continues to rub her forearm, with hypnotic persistence.

She screams. It's horrible. A hateful idea. I don't want It to happen like that.

Now you're getting all excited about nothing. Let me give you one of those pills that the Swiss doctor.

No!

But she eventually swallows the pill and soon she is feeling sleepy and wholly dissociated from all that he has planned for her, as though Pearl, who once could do It and now can no longer do It, is someone totally different from this Pearl spread-eagled on the rumpled double bed in the Barcelona hotel.

The next day they go to the dentist, who is furry and agile, his simian mouth cracking open in repeated smiles that reveal his gold inlays, as though to say, See how rich I am, here is all my treasure! He gives her an injection in her arm that makes her feel even more sleepy and dissociated than the pills of the night before, and then he gives her two injections in the mouth. The drilling and placing of the gold filling and the rectifier crystal take a long time and the dentist mutters imprecations under his breath in a language that is common to him and Krishna but that Pearl cannot understand. At one point he drops the tiny amplifier and the two men go on their hands and knees, two monkeys in quest of a fallen nut. They are now far more agitated than she.

Pearl is lying motionless in the chair, a tear glistening on either nacreous cheekbone.

At one point she says, I don't want.

But the two men appear not to hear her.

5

After that there were times when she forgot that It had gone from her and that her only gift was Krishna's gift of the ingenious piece of metal hidden under a toothcap. When the voices now came to her, she hardly noticed that they had grown oddly blurred, ebbing and flowing as though brought to her on wave after wave of some invisible but circumambient sea. Even her fear of being found out began to recede and she no longer awoke, sweating and with furiously thumping heart, in the loneliness of hotel bedrooms with Krishna asleep beside her, to think, Some day someone will realize. And then no one will ever believe that once I could really do It. They'll say that I always had Krishna to help me. They'll say we always cheated.

Krishna told her, we've only substituted one miracle for another, my dear. My miracle is every bit as extraordinary as your miracle, you know. They were growing very rich.

Krishna used to laugh at all the scientists. They just don't know how to observe, he would say. Conjurors know. But scientists are children. Worse than children. Even children observe more. She frowned in bewilderment and he went on, In the world of science most people are trying to prove the truth of a hypothesis to which they are already committed. The hypothesis is more important to them than any evidence.

Only once is Pearl convinced that someone who claims to

believe that she can do It, really does not do so. He is a short,
shrill American television personality, with spidery over-active
hands and popping eyes and she appears on a series of his shows
that are concerned with the paranormal. He holds her so tightly
by the elbow that later that evening, in her New York hotel
bedroom, she finds bruises on the nacreous skin. His breath is
slightly sour as his face approaches hers and she notices that
there is a faint rash on his forehead, just below the hairline. He
talks very fast and from time to time stalks about among the
audience, followed by the cameras, like some hungry, im-
passioned animal in an invisible cage.

There are gasps of amazement from the people packed before
her. He exclaims, Fantastic! Incredible! Extraordinary! The
scientists nod their heads ruefully and one says, Well, you've
got me beaten. I've seen nothing like this, says another.

But when he says goodbye to her, taking her cold hand in his
sweating one, the famous interviewer gives her a glance of
sardonic complicity. He silently seems to be telling her, We're
both fakes. We understand each other. That glance frightens
her and makes her feel ashamed. She does not wish to have any
community with that shrill, prancing, self-intoxicated figure.

He guessed something, she tells Krishna as she slips out of her
dress.

Nonsense. You were perfect. I was perfect too.

He guessed something.

Not a chance. But thank God no one suggested total body
X-radiation again. Krishna has had to refuse that twice – at
Göttingen University and at Heidelberg University. The
Germans are so thorough.

6

Now there are months of success even wilder than in that period
when she really could do It, and Krishna is delighted with her.
She grows even more etiolated, thinner, vaguer; but he tells her
that once they have got through this year ahead of them, then

they'll take off on a holiday, perhaps a cruise round the world (they have already circled the world more than once). But before that they will marry. She wonders why he keeps putting off something that they could do any afternoon. Perhaps back in India he has a wife and children? But she does not want to think about that.

Then something strange and alarming begins to happen. She is asleep after lunch in preparation for an appearance on Rome television and Krishna has told her that he must go out for a breath of air. Suddenly she is roused by the sound of voices, there in her head. But she has not activated the tiny amplifier and it is unlikely that Krishna has activated his tiny transmitter. She listens, aghast, to a woman whom she does not know and a man whom she does.

What's she doing? (The voice is American.)

What she usually does. Sleeping. I've never known anyone who sleeps so much.

It must take it out of her.

Well, I suppose so. But living with her takes it out of me. Thank God, there's you to put it back.

Why on earth did you ever take up with her?

I often ask myself that question. But, oh well, it's fascinating. In its way.

And lucrative.

And lucrative.

She doesn't want to listen to the voices of the woman that she does not know and the man that she does. But on and on they go, there inside her head. She cannot stop them. She cannot sleep.

When Krishna comes back she does not tell him that she has listened to the whole atrocious conversation; but she says, I have a feeling that there's something wrong with this thing in my mouth.

What do you mean?

Well, from time to time I . . . hear things.

Hear things?

Scraps of conversation.

He pooh-poohs that as he combs his long, sleek hair before the mirror. He combs the hair as though it belonged to someone whom he loved, with long, languorous strokes from the crown of his head to the glistening ends. Impossible, he says. You can't hear anything unless I'm transmitting.

She shrugs in resigned agreement. But intermittently she goes on hearing scraps of conversation between him and other people. She learns the full extent of his contempt for her, even loathing. She cannot sleep, becomes hysterical, on one occasion even makes a half-hearted effort to cut her wrists with one of his razor blades. Finally knowing that she is no use to him or to anyone in her present state, he agrees that yes, they'll have the implant removed. They go to Barcelona and once again the agile, furry dentist gives her an injection in her arm and two injections in her mouth. This is the end, baby, Krishna says. After this we're washed up. Since he met that unknown American woman, he has begun to talk in these Americanisms.

7

But it wasn't the end but only a rebeginning. Where once there had been Krishna's device, there was now a clumsy amalgam filling; but she could again do It. Even when she did not want to do It, she would hear the conversations; not only Krishna and the American woman, or Krishna and auntie and mother, or auntie and mother between themselves, but also a host of other people, in whom she had no interest but who insisted on making themselves audible to her. Like actual physical masses, the identities of all these anonymous others pressed on her and crushed her. She could hardly breathe for them.

Did you really have that horrible thing removed?

Yes, of course I did. And now by some miracle the gift has come back to you. What could be better than that?

Silence, she might have answered. But she did not do so, since now she had grown afraid of losing him. As long as she could do It, he would never leave her.

At any time of the day or night the voices now torment her, a babbling murmur that slowly rises to a crescendo in her head, as though a hibernating swarm of bees had been stirred into angry life. But still the two whizz about the world, the pallid girl and her pantherine 'manager', and more and more people acclaim her, Astonishing, Marvellous, Incredible, Miraculous.

In a Tokyo hotel she refuses to go to a party, given by one diplomat and his wife and attended by a number of other diplomats and their wives, even though Krishna tells her, You've got to go. The party's for *us*. Don't you understand? All those people will be coming for us.

But she clutches her head, that head that is now ceaselessly throbbing with the insistent identities of others, and cries out, I can't, can't, can't! All I want is some peace. Some peace, some peace.

He knots his black tie and arranges the handkerchief in his breast pocket. He is angry with her, she knows that, but he says nothing of his anger. I'll have to go. It'll be better than nothing. Then he adds roughly from the door, For God's sake, now pull yourself together. It's no fun being with you, you know. They have not made love for a long time. He walks out into the late violet dusk, smelling so strongly of scent that the diplomat who is his host will later say to his wife in bed, Dreadful man, that. Reeking of some bazaar perfume. Did you notice?

Pearl lies on the bed in the gathering darkness and one by one the voices creep into her head. At first they are English or American.

Oh, I feel so.
Oh, I want so.
But of course I.
But of course you.
Well, yes if.
Well, no if.
Oh, I wish I.
I wish.
I wish.

Then there are other voices, French voices, German voices, Italian voices, even Japanese voices. The whole hotel is talking in her head. Her head tries to contain them all but it is not big enough. Her head will burst.

She jumps off the bed and goes to the window, holding back the curtain with a fragile hand as she peers out. The violet dusk has now deepened to night. Opposite the hotel, they are excavating the foundations for another, even more expensive hotel, a skyscraper. The men are working on under arc-lights that reveal their puny, half-naked bodies. From here they look so small, so very small; but their voices in her head are loud, so very loud. Everyone else in the hotel has been complaining about a huge machine that rhythmically thumps on the earth with a terrifying tremor. But the voices are so noisy that she can hardly hear it. She sees it, however. Up and down goes its giant's hammer, up and down, and the men swarm about it.

She pulls on her coat over her underclothes and she goes out. She runs into the street and she then runs across it. The voices are getting louder; that vein is throbbing at one corner of her forehead; the wind is blowing, hot and dry, against her fragile throat. One of the puny men, who is in fact not puny at all, sees her and attempts to grab her. But before he can do so her head and the voices inside it have been thumped into the dust by that giant's hammer, to be silenced forever.

Her suicide horrifies everyone in Europe and America but secretly delights the Japanese.

They are, after all, connoisseurs of that kind of thing.